Nurse in Doubt

Rose Williams

Thorndike Press   **Chivers Press**
Waterville, Maine USA   **Bath, England**

This Large Print edition is published by Thorndike Press®, USA and by Chivers Press, England.

Published in 2003 in the U.S. by arrangement with Maureen Moran Agency.

Published in 2003 in the U.K. by arrangement with the author.

U.S. Softcover 0-7862-5705-9 (Paperback)
U.K. Hardcover 0-7540-7345-9 (Chivers Large Print)
U.K. Softcover 0-7540-7346-7 (Camden Large Print)

The text of this Large Print edition is unabridged.
Other aspects of the book may vary from the original edition.

Set in 16 pt. Plantin by Myrna S. Raven.

Printed in the United States on permanent paper.

British Library Cataloguing-in-Publication Data available

Library of Congress Cataloging-in-Publication Data

Williams, Rose, 1912–
      Nurse in doubt / by Rose Williams.
            p.   cm.   2003137 7
      ISBN 0-7862-5705-9 (lg. print : sc : alk. paper)
      1. Nurses — Fiction.   2. Physicians — Fiction.
      3. Stepmothers — Fiction.   4. Inheritance and succession
      — Fiction.   5. Large type books.   I. Title.
      PR9199.3.R5996N79 2003
      813′.54—dc21   2003053013

Nurse in Doubt

Chapter One

It was just a little after seven on a warm July evening when Edna pushed open the screen door of the rambling, brown-shingled house and stepped out on the porch. She stood there for a few minutes on the porch, a troubled expression on her even-featured, intelligent face. She was not an extravagantly pretty girl, but there was a sensitivity mirrored in her features, and this was accentuated by her large brown eyes.

Just now her eyes showed concern. She clasped the porch column with her hand and stared into the empty street. It was a quiet time of the evening, and there in the shade of the giant elm trees that had guarded the old house through much of its eighty-year history, she felt her tensions ease. With a sigh the dark-haired girl moved on down the porch steps and gave her attention to the hedge of roses that lined either side of the short cement walk leading to the street.

Her father had planted these rosebushes some years ago, and she still took an interest and pride in their care. They were part of the past that seemed so wonderful to her now that her father was dead and she found herself sharing the house with Bernice.

There was a sound from behind the screen door, and she looked up toward the porch with slightly startled eyes. She could just see the shadow of her stepmother's tall figure behind the screening.

In a slightly complaining tone, Bernice said "Oh, you're at the roses again!"

Edna wondered why her stepmother resented her giving the bushes the care they so obviously needed. It apparently was because any reminder of her late husband seemed to upset her.

"They need some pruning," Edna said. "I may as well finish it tonight."

"I suppose so." Bernice tried to sound casual but didn't quite cover the doubt in her tone. Her shadow vanished from behind the screen.

With a real sense of relief Edna turned to her task. Earlier in the afternoon, when she'd first come home after working the day shift at the hospital, she'd spent a short while pruning the fast-growing hedge. Then she'd left it to do some ironing and get dinner ready. Bernice nearly always managed to be away until it was just time to sit down at the table. Today had been no exception. Her stepmother had arrived in the gaudy red convertible of one of the actors at the summer playhouse at a minute or two before six.

Edna had been afraid she might have to cope with an unexpected guest, as Bernice seldom hesitated to extend invitations to her many friends. Luckily, tonight Bernice had been in the company of Elliot Roger, the stock company leading man, and he never stayed for a meal. So there had been no problems at dinner, except for her stepmother's continual complaining. Bernice, who could be so charming and gay whenever strangers were around, reserved a private mood of caustic annoyance for Edna.

Bending down to pick up her work gloves and shears, the thin, dark-haired girl felt that she'd endured about all she could. If Bernice kept on as she had been doing for the past weeks, she'd have to leave. Probably that was what her stepmother wanted. The only thing that held Edna back was that leaving would mean more than just going away from her father's house. It would mean leaving her job at the hospital and going to another town. People in Farmingham would talk if she moved to her uncle's or took a place of her own. The town, which was just under twenty thousand, was small enough so that everyone pretty much knew everyone else's business. Edna had no wish to become a victim of the town gossips again. She'd gone through enough of that.

She began using the large shears to trim places along the hedge where it had grown at an unruly pace. As she worked, she recalled the unpleasantness that Bernice had caused at dinner.

As usual, her stepmother had begun with references to her work. "I can't understand why you ever wanted to be a nurse," Bernice had said with disgust in her voice. "I should think a young girl like you would want a job with more life."

Edna had controlled her anger. "I like nursing," she said simply, not looking up from her plate. "We enjoy our work. It's fun being part of the team at the hospital."

Bernice had looked at her as if she went out of her mind. "Don't tell me that," she said firmly. "I've been around there enough to know that most of it is plain drudgery."

Bernice had taken on the work of hospital aide as one of her social chores. She rarely showed up, but her occasional rare appearances had served to make her an authority on everything pertaining to the Farmingham General Hospital. Edna knew that her stepmother had volunteered for the work only because it gave her a chance to mingle with some of the town's socialites who would normally certainly have avoided her.

"I feel the same way about it as Uncle Charles does," Edna told her stepmother across the table. "I like doing a worthwhile job. So many professions are completely pointless."

Bernice gave her a nasty smile. "You don't need to remind me that your Uncle Charles is head of the hospital," she said. "I'm well aware of it, even if I'm not much impressed. He's really not much more practical than your father was."

Now she's really on her favorite subject, Edna thought grimly.

"Charles Brayley may be the hospital superintendent and the best surgeon we have here," Bernice continued, "but he is not a practical man. Naturally, he's not as bad as your father." Her stepmother paused to sigh. "Why I ever married an artist!"

"I don't think Daddy did so badly," Edna defended him stoutly. "He paid my way through private school and spent a small fortune restoring this old house."

"Money wasted!" Bernice said bitterly. "If I had the cash he spent on this monstrosity, I'd be far away from Farmingham now!"

"It's a lovely old place," Edna told her. "And Daddy left enough paintings to sell for quite a few years, and money in the bank for both of us as well."

Bernice shook her head. "Don't tell me about our bank balance. I know all about it, to my sorrow. We've just barely enough to scrimp by on if we live like church mice."

Edna found herself laughing at this. The comparison of the flashy Bernice to a church mouse was just too much. She said: "I think we're managing very nicely. And if you could get even a part-time job —"

"You know that's impossible," Bernice interrupted her. "I was a private secretary, and there are no jobs available in this town that I'd consider. Anyway, I haven't been well since your father died."

This was another of Bernice's fond imaginings. But Edna knew from experience there was no point extending the argument to cover the wide range of her stepmother's supposed health problems.

Bernice lit a cigarette and rose from the table with her coffee. "Edna, you simply do not have the respect you should for me," she announced, and stalked out to the living room to sit alone.

Edna relaxed a little. Glancing up at the large portrait of her father that decorated one of the wood-paneled walls and dominated the room, she studied the rueful expression on his gentle artist's face and wondered if it were due to the perceptive talent of the artist who had painted it or if it had come about as a result of listening to Bernice's endless diatribes.

Staring at the portrait with her large, solemn brown eyes, Edna whispered for perhaps the hundredth time: "Why did you do it, Daddy? How could you have fallen in love with her?"

The answer came echoing back from a three-year memory, when her father had confronted her one winter evening before the fireplace with the news. He had looked even more tired than usual.

"I hope you won't find this too difficult to understand," he'd said slowly. "After all these years since your mother died, I find myself wanting to marry again."

She hadn't as yet met Bernice, and she'd touched his arm gently, eager for his happiness. "I think it's wonderful news, Dad," she'd told him.

13

He'd stared at her, still vaguely disturbed. "I hope you'll always feel that way about it," he said. "This girl, Bernice, is the secretary of a wealthy man who has bought a number of my paintings."

His mention of his proposed wife as a girl startled her a bit.

"Bernice is only five years older than you, my dear," her father had continued. Edna had tried to hide her surprise. Since she was twenty-two, it meant her stepmother would be a mere twenty-seven!

She managed a smile. "She's very young! You must have made a real conquest!"

Her fifty-year-old father had shrugged and half-turned from her. "I'm very fond of her," he said with a slight tremor in his voice; "too fond to listen to my own reason. I have the feeling she will be good for me, good for my work."

In a way Bernice had been good for his work. He'd gone at his painting with renewed enthusiasm. In his absorption with his new bride and his heavy schedule of new work, he'd either ignored or not been aware of the scandal the marriage caused in Farmingham.

Edna had borne the brunt of it. She'd smiled her way through endless hours of questions and knowing, snide remarks. In the end the bride from the city was almost accepted. Not quite, but almost.

Of course Bernice didn't help the situation any. Her tall, leggy frame was continually draped in the most outlandish of new fashions. She dressed by fad rather than taste. Her square-faced blonde beauty was vivid if slightly vulgar, and she had a knack of brushing people the wrong way. She made few real friends.

As a result she became bitter and complaining. Within a year and a half of the marriage, Edna's father was found, paintbrush still in hand, stretched on the floor by his easel, where he'd been stricken while working feverishly on a special portrait assignment. He never rallied.

Edna listened as her father's will was read. The house was left for both women to use. There was no provision for its sale. The money and paintings were divided between them. So Edna and this blonde girl only a few years older than herself had settled down to a life of hostility in the big, lonely house.

Edna found surcease from the pain of her father's unexpected death by throwing herself into her nursing with new dedication. She'd also been given comfort and love by her Uncle Charles and his wife.

15

And just lately she'd met Jim Boone.

Bernice had carried on at a dizzy pace. Within a few months of her husband's death, she had started the town gossips going by her frequent dates with young men her own age. Edna saw no real harm in this, but it did present a problem in diplomacy.

Her stepmother flaunted her actions without any attempt to consider Edna's position. "I'm a young woman," she'd announced. "I'm not going to spend the rest of my life in widow's weeds!"

As time passed, the situation became accepted. Bernice complained about her income being inadequate but made no attempt to find work. Instead, she began devoting her time to a number of social activities. This included her role as a hospital aide, also her position on the sponsoring committees of the summer theatre and of the symphony orchestra in the winter.

Edna somehow found herself coping with the unpleasant reality of her new life, but it was becoming increasingly difficult. Bernice had even been jealous of her friendship with Jim Boone, although she'd pretended to approve of it.

The Boone family spent their summers at a big estate just outside Farmingham.

They had been coming to Maine for years, and Edna had once worked at a summer hotel with the tall, rather handsome Jim when they were both just out of high school.

Horace Boone was nationally known for his large pharmaceutical house. His drug business was a family inheritance and had long outgrown its humble beginning as a patent medicine firm. He was a stout, balding man, seldom seen in Farmingham, although he did come down for weekends. His wife was dead, and his household was run by a sister. There were two sons, Jim and a younger brother Eric. Eric was a junior in college and had the reputation around Farmingham of being a reckless playboy. His sports car was low-slung and white and lent a frenzied glamour to the small town's streets.

Jim was more serious and already in business with his father. He and Edna had met at the hospital when his father had been a patient there for a few days because of a recurrence of an asthmatic condition. They recalled their friendship at the summer hotel, and soon they were dating on a regular basis.

Bernice's reaction had been completely as expected. "I don't know why you waste time on him," she sniffed. "He'll never marry you."

Edna's face had crimsoned. "I'm not thinking about marriage and neither is he," she'd retorted angrily. "We're merely friends!"

Bernice had made a face. "I've heard that story before!" she observed.

One of the liabilities of having a step-mother close to your own age was the fact that she was almost always bound to be jealous of your male friends, Edna decided. She tried to keep her occasional young men out of Bernice's sight, especially Jim Boone.

Tonight she was meeting Jim, and they were attending the summer theatre together. She'd arranged to meet him at a downtown corner, even though he'd wanted to drive by the house and pick her up.

She had worked her way along the hedge until she was near the sidewalk when a dark sedan came up alongside the curb and stopped. A moment later, a slim, bald man wearing gold-rimmed glasses got out and came across the sidewalk to greet her with a smile.

"How's my girl tonight?" he asked, giving her a playful hug with one arm. It was her Uncle Charles, hospital superintendent and chief surgeon.

She smiled at him as she pulled off her gloves. "I wasn't expecting you tonight," she said.

"I didn't expect to be up this way myself," he replied. "But I received word my new assistant is arriving tomorrow, and I had to make final arrangements for his living quarters. I've located a nice bachelor apartment right round the corner."

Edna showed interest. "Really! Then we'll be having him for a neighbor. What's his name?"

"Preston Halliday," her uncle said. "Son of an old colleague of mine. He's been working in the research field. Had positions with several of the top places, but for some reason he wants to make a change. Soon as I heard about it, I used all my influence to try to get him to come here. I finally managed it."

She nodded. "Well done! But does he know what he's in for? Farmingham isn't exactly a big medical center. And our hospital isn't the largest or best equipped in the state. Do you think he'll be satisfied?"

Her Uncle Charles stared at her with a slight frown on his round face. "I assume he knows we're not a large hospital," he said. "One thing is certain: he didn't ask any questions. I had the impression he was willing to take anything that offered a change."

"It's not often you find research men leaving their field," Edna said. "I wonder what his reason is."

Her uncle shrugged. "We'll find out in good time. You'll be meeting him tomorrow." Then, changing the subject, "By the way, the last report was that the gastrectomy I did this morning is coming along handsomely."

"I saw him in the recovery room," Edna said. "I was surprised you managed the operation in such a short time."

"It wasn't a complete removal," he told her. "It didn't take quite three hours. I've had them run a lot longer than that when there were complications."

"I'm glad he's doing well," Edna said. "I know they were worried about him because of his heart."

"He's had a condition for some years," her uncle agreed. "But there was no point in delaying the operation, since he had to have it. The risk is minimal these days, what with modern methods and anesthesia."

"Edna!" It was Bernice calling from the porch.

Edna turned and saw her stepmother standing there, looking stunningly lovely in a simple white dress that brought out her vivid blonde beauty. Before she had a chance to answer, Bernice saw Charles Brayley and hurried down the porch steps to meet him with a disarming smile.

"Dr. Brayley," she beamed on him, "how nice of you to come visit us!"

He looked slightly uncomfortable. "Actually, it isn't a visit. I was passing by and saw Edna and decided on impulse to have a chat."

Edna asked: "Did you want me for something?" A shadow crossed the smiling face of her stepmother. "Yes, I did. I had a phone call just now from Jim Boone. He asked me to tell you he'd be a few minutes late." Bernice's blue eyes were sad as they studied her. "You didn't tell me you were meeting Jim tonight," she said with a sigh.

"No, I didn't," Edna answered in a quiet voice, dismissing the suggestion that she might have been expected to.

There was an awkward moment of silence, during which Bernice recaptured her too sunny smile. "Edna likes to keep secrets," she told Charles Brayley.

With a knowing glance at Edna, he said:

"I'd hardly call Jim a secret. He and Edna are old friends."

"So I understand," Bernice said airily. "Of course I tell her she's seeing the wrong brother. I think that Eric is the interesting one. And I adore his sports car."

Dr. Brayley regarded his sister-in-law with amazement. "I don't know that I share your enthusiasm. He's a little too careless about stop streets for my liking. I almost found myself in a collision with him the other day."

"A bit high-spirited," the blonde woman agreed. "But then, I like to see a young man with some life."

Charles Brayley glanced at his wrist-watch. "I have to go. I have some things to finish at the hospital." He smiled in the direction of Bernice. "The new assistant superintendent is arriving in the morning."

"Is that so!" She was all interest. "I'd heard you had a new man coming."

"Yes," Charles Brayley said. "We've needed someone for several months."

"I don't see why you didn't give the appointment to Dr. Rodman," Bernice said. "I think he'd be ideal for the position."

Edna enjoyed her uncle's expression of horror. She knew how he felt about Dr. William Rodman. He was bound to be upset by Bernice's endorsement of the squat, ugly little poseur. Dr. William Rodman had arrived in Farmingham a little more than ten years ago. He was a middle-aged man who boasted of a fantastically successful practice he'd sacrificed on the West Coast because his wife preferred New England. Word gradually filtered back to Farmingham that his practice in California had been in an obscure town where he'd not been highly regarded by either the community or the profession. But he had a good bedside manner, and only a few people knew the true story of his background, so he prospered.

Almost at once every neurotic female in Farmingham clamored for his attention. Dr. Rodman proved an expert at giving them the sort of representation of a dedicated physician they'd grown used to on television.

His practice grew rapidly, to the dismay of the other doctors. It was good that the majority of his patients required nothing more than simple medication. In the few instances where he'd attempted to treat seriously ill people, he had had some alarming failures along with a few lucky successes. Of course the successes were quoted as examples of his genius by his admiring female clientele, while the hospital board considered seriously whether or not they should still give him access to their facilities.

Somehow he hung on. His ugly little figure in a long white gown, a pince-nez with black ribbon perched on his button nose, was the signal for concealed giggles on the part of the hospital's student nurses. Superintendent Charles Brayley and his serious-minded colleagues more frequently greeted the eccentric doctor with scowls.

Edna watched her Uncle Charles swallow hard as he said: "I can't agree with you completely as to his suitability. In my case, I believe he is doing far too well in private practice to consider taking a staff position."

Bernice was happily impervious to the insinuation and said: "I suppose so. Who is this new man? Somebody from out of town?"

Dr. Brayley nodded. "Yes. That's how I came to be up here tonight. I found him an apartment around the corner. You'll be having him as a neighbor."

The blonde woman's eyes brightened. "Really? How interesting. I suppose you had trouble getting him an apartment, es-

24

pecially if he has young children."

Edna found herself admiring Bernice's technique for getting information.

Her uncle smiled. "Actually, he's a bachelor, so there was no problem. I've gotten him a nice little place, all furnished. His name, by the way, is Dr. Preston Halliday. He's been working in the research field."

"He sounds interesting," Bernice commented. "I'll look forward to seeing him. I think our group is having a meeting at the hospital tomorrow."

Charles Brayley looked at her with some amusement. "Quite possibly. I'm afraid I'm not too well acquainted with the meeting dates of the hospital organizations. But if you do come down, no doubt he'll be introduced to your group."

After a few minutes more of generalities, he wished them good night and drove away. When he was out of sight, Bernice turned to Edna.

"Jim said he was taking you to the theatre."

"Yes, he is," Edna started up the walk to the house.

Bernice followed and commented: "I wish you had let me know earlier. I want to go over there one night, and I could have gotten a lift with you two."

Edna avoided a reply. Hastily she made her way upstairs and took a quick shower.

Afterward she selected a green crepe dress that was stylishly simple and a single strand of white pearls, a white bag and a white sweater for use later when it was colder.

Bernice was on the phone talking to someone as she left. A few minutes later she found Jim parked by the busy corner where they'd arranged to meet.

The blond young man opened the car door for her with a harassed smile on his good-natured face. "Don't do this to me again, darling," he begged. "I've had a policeman breathing down my neck for the last five minutes. I thought he was going to give me a ticket."

She smiled. "Sorry. I'll do better next time."

"I'll consider that a promise." He laughed and swung the car into the regular traffic lane. "I could have picked you up at the house. Your stepmother seemed to think it strange you were meeting me down here."

"You know stepmothers!" Edna said. "And you could have guessed I'd be late. It's the garden season, and I'm our only gardener."

Chapter Two

Mornings were always cool in Farmingham even during the summer months. Before Edna left the house, she put on a light blue summer coat over her crisp, white uniform. She let herself out quietly so as not to disturb Bernice.

For almost a year she'd arrived at the hospital in time to get her orange juice, toast and coffee before going on duty. Usually she had it with Mel Parker, a nurse about her own age. This was a bright, pleasant morning and gave promise of a sunny day.

When she entered the small cafeteria with its light green walls, there were already a few groups scattered at various tables. Mel was waiting for her near the door where they always sat.

She languidly waved a hand which held a cigarette. "I was beginning to think you weren't going to make it." She was a thin girl, with mousy blonde hair and a rather pretty face spoiled by too prominent cheek bones. Her most interesting features were her eyes, which were bright blue and flashed continually with cynical good humor.

Edna seated herself and slipped off her coat. "I was late getting in," she admitted with a smile. "We went to the summer theatre and then for some dancing at the hotel afterward."

"Ah, youth, youth!" Mel observed her with mock admiration. "How I wish I had it to enjoy again! Last night I had a very gay time. I washed my hair and put in curlers and read the latest issue of *True Romance*."

Edna laughed. "Well, you did gain something. Your hair looks a good deal better than mine this morning." She got up. "I'd better look after my tray or I will be late."

She hurried to the counter and helped herself to juice, toast and coffee, then went back to join Mel at the table.

Mel gave her an amused look as she sat down. "I trust the redoubtable Jim was suitably romantic last evening?"

"I was late meeting him and he almost got a parking ticket," Edna said with a laugh. "But he soon got over his annoyance and we did have a good evening."

"Jim is a nice boy." Mel ground out her cigarette. "It's a wonder to me your dear stepmother hasn't tried to grasp him in her lovely paws."

Edna gave a knowing smile. "She's not above it," she said. "But I have taken precautions to keep him a safe distance from the delectable Bernice."

"Wise girl," Mel approved.

"At the moment Bernice is excited by the news we're getting a new doctor," Edna went on. "Uncle Charles dropped by last night and accidentally mentioned that he had found him an apartment near our place. Bernice was instantly intrigued."

"Her romantic ideas!" Mel rolled her eyes. "Bernice on the prowl is a wicked adversary. But I thought she had a favorite medico — Dr. William Rodman."

"She got in a good word about him to Uncle Charles. Said she thought he should have been made the new assistant superintendent."

Mel chuckled. "I'd loved to have seen your uncle's face when she told him that."

Edna gave an amused nod. "It was something. He got off the hook by saying he was sure Dr. Rodman was doing too well in private practice."

Mel stood. "Nice going for Uncle Charles. By the way, guess whom we've got

29

as a patient on our floor? Came in last evening."

Edna shrugged. "Could be anyone."

"Someone very important," Mel told her. "David Danton, the Broadway columnist. He's in for a series of tests."

Edna raised her eyebrows. "What's he doing in a Farmingham hospital? He's a New Yorker."

"Yes, but his brother summers down here. They have that big brick house along the cliff. And David Danton and his wife have been spending the holidays with him."

"I still don't understand it," Edna said. "I should think he'd want to be looked after in New York."

"Don't short-change your Uncle Charles," Mel reminded her. "He has a lot of patients coming here from all over the place. And your prospective father-in-law is among them. I understand the mighty Horace is due back this week for some more help for that asthmatic condition."

"Jim mentioned that last night," Edna agreed. "I guess he's been having a hard time trying to rest."

"I hear they're worried about his heart," Mel said. "One thing certain: their worry can't be that it's too large. No one has ever accused him of that." She winked as she left.

Edna smiled. It was common gossip in Farmingham that the elder Boone was very tight-fisted. Neither of his sons had this failing. Jim was not a spendthrift, but he certainly hadn't shown himself to be mean about money.

And his brother, Eric, was as wildly careless about money as he was about everything else. People shook their heads and grinned when they talked about Eric, but it wasn't funny for Jim and the rest of the family. Edna knew they were extremely worried about the wildly irresponsible young man. At the moment he was carrying on a flaming romance with a petite, redheaded charmer who was the leading lady at the local summer theatre.

He had been standing in the back of the theatre when she had gone in with Jim last night. As they stood waiting to be ushered to their seats, he had come over to them, handsome and a few inches taller than his older brother.

"Nancy is great in this show." He smiled at Edna. "I haven't missed a performance."

She had heard the rumor that he bought a seat for every performance. She said: "We naturally expect you to be enthusiastic. I'll tell you what I think afterward."

Eric laughed. "All right. Make up your own mind."

The play was "Mary, Mary," and the redhead turned out to be a very fine little actress. On the way out, Jim had paused to tell his brother: "I think you've picked a winner this time. She's great!"

Edna had added her praise, and Eric had looked delighted.

"I'd like to have you meet her," he told them. "They've got a late run-through of the next play scheduled tonight, or we could all go some place together."

There was no question that the young man had fallen in love with the actress. Edna hoped it would work out well for both of them. She gathered up her purse and coat and left the cafeteria to go upstairs.

She was working on the third floor, and Mel was also there on the same shift. As she reported to the desk, she saw the blonde girl opening the drug cabinet to prepare a medication. Mel glanced across at her and winked.

The head nurse on the floor was a middle-aged woman with graying hair. She had come back to nursing to help send her two sons to college. She could be both severe and demanding, but she was an efficient supervisor whom they all respected. Now she glanced up from her desk at Edna, giving her a sharp scrutiny from behind her heavy horn-rimmed glasses.

"I hope you're feeling energetic today, Brayley," she began. "We haven't an empty room on the floor."

"I'd rather have it that way." Edna smiled. "It doesn't give you time to think about being tired."

Emma Graham gave a small grunt in reply. It was neither approving nor disapproving, but indicated that Edna might feel differently about a crowded floor if she were a few years older and the supervisor.

Mrs. Graham nodded in the direction of the first of several corridors that extended like spokes of a wheel from the central desk at which she sat. "We have a new patient in 353," she said. "David Danton, the columnist. He has some further tests this morning. Perhaps you'd better start with him."

Edna nodded and made her way briskly down the hall to 353. The door to the private room was slightly ajar, and when she entered she found David Danton standing with his back to the door as he looked out the big window that took in the skyline of Farmingham and the coast and bay beyond.

Hearing her come in, he turned and

smiled. She recognized him from his appearances on television. But he looked different from what she had expected. He was gaunt, with large circles under his friendly eyes. His pleasant if rather weak face had a blue coating of beard, and his thinning gray hair had not been combed.

Seeing her, he brushed it roughly across his bald dome. "I'm afraid I'm not too presentable," he apologized.

"For a patient in a hospital, I'd say you're doing very well." Edna smiled as she picked up his chart. "At least you're not on your back."

"Actually I'm a sort of fraud," he said. "I'm in here for tests. So I'm hardly in the regular patient class."

She studied his chart as he spoke, noting the pleasant low masculinity of his voice that had been one of his main assets on television. Of course he wrote well, in addition. She saw that he was scheduled for X-rays in a half-hour.

She smiled at him and put the chart back on the bed. "You've had breakfast, I suppose?"

He returned the smile. "Earliest in years. This room has been a little like Grand Hotel, with people coming and going every minute."

"And now I'm here to bother you," she said.

"A pleasure," Danton assured her. "I don't know where this hospital finds so many pretty nurses."

She gave him a warning shake of the head as she prepared a thermometer and held it ready. "I'm afraid flattery won't help. Hadn't you better sit down or get into bed until we go through the necessary procedures?"

David Danton gave her a comic look of dismay. "I'll sit down," he said. "I have a horror of hospital beds. People are always dying in them."

Edna laughed. "A lot of people die just walking down the street."

The columnist gave a small shudder. "How did we get started on this pleasant subject so early in the day? Just put it down to my natural dislike of hospitals."

"Then we'd better get you out of here as soon as possible," she told him as she placed the thermometer in his mouth.

There was a short silence as she waited to read the results. When she'd finished, she said: "There. You can have the room to yourself for a while. Then you're due downstairs for X-rays."

He glanced up at her with a wan smile.

"I'm not in that much of a hurry to get rid of you. It's just that I find this routine a bit frightening."

"They should finish with you in a few days," she assured him. "Haven't you been feeling well?"

"A bit liverish." He sighed. "I've lost my appetite, and I have trouble swallowing. Several times in restaurants I've had to get up from the table and leave. I'm almost afraid to go anywhere and order a dinner now. I'm never certain I'll be able to get through it. At home I eat nothing much but soup. Ethel, my wife, said she was sick of making it for me continually and I had to do something about it. So here I am!"

Edna listened to his story and wondered why he had come to this small town hospital rather than consult some specialist in New York. She said: "So you've had trouble for some time. Didn't you talk to your New York doctor?"

David Danton's gaunt face took on an embarrassed expression. "He's always making mountains out of molehills," he murmured. "I decided to have my condition checked down here on the quiet. I'm pretty well known, you see, and I dislike publicity."

She nodded. "And in New York news

about personalities gets around quickly."

"That's it," he said. "I'm much happier to be treated here."

She paused at the door with a smile. "I'm sure we'll soon have you well again. If you need anything, you can press the light for me."

"Fine," the columnist said. "I've some papers ordered. Will you see they are sent in here as soon as they arrive?"

"I'll look after it myself," Edna promised. As she left her patient, he had opened a book on his lap and seemed prepared to read awhile.

She had a convalescent appendectomy case to look after and an elderly woman with a broken hip who required an alcohol rub. After that she gave some medication to the seriously ill diabetic who had recently had her leg amputated. It was not until David Danton passed her on his way to the elevator with a nurse from the X-ray department that she had a chance to catch her breath for a moment. The gaunt man smiled at her in passing.

Head Nurse Graham, observing this, asked: "What do you make of him?"

"He seems very nice."

"He is," Mrs. Graham agreed. "But what do you make of his condition?"

"It's hard to say," Edna observed. "He seems awfully nervous. Of course many people do feel that way about hospitals."

"I know," Mrs. Graham agreed. "One of my boys says he hates the smell of hospitals. I told him there wasn't such a thing as a particular hospital smell. But he just said I'd been around it too long to notice. But there's more than just a dislike of hospitals in the case of Mr. David Danton. I think he's badly frightened."

Edna nodded. "Probably. Patients try to diagnose themselves too often. They start to imagine all kinds of dreadful things."

"That's our Mr. Danton's trouble, I'm sure," the head nurse said.

Mel Parker came up to the desk with a worried expression and interrupted their discussion. "I'm having trouble with that girl with the thyroidectomy. She's complaining that she can't breathe."

Mrs. Graham raised her eyebrows. "What's her heart rate?"

Mel said: "It's down to about forty beats a minute."

The head nurse turned to the phone. "I'll see if Dr. Rodman is in the building. She's one of his patients."

"Worse luck for her," Mel said to Edna. "That's why she's in this fix. He'll try to blame it all on your uncle, since he did the operating."

Mrs. Graham gave Mel a reproving glance. Then she spoke into the phone again. "Very well. I wish you'd ask him to come up to his patient on the third floor as soon as possible." She put down the receiver. "He'll be up in a few minutes. And please don't let me hear you giving any more personal opinions about Dr. Rodman, Miss Parker."

Mel looked aggrieved and hurried off on another errand. Edna was still filling in charts at the desk when Dr. Rodman stepped off the elevator. The ugly little bald man approached the desk with his usual slick smile.

"Good morning, ladies," he greeted them in his pompous way. "They tell me you have a problem."

Head Nurse Graham nodded. "Your thyroidectomy patient, Doctor. Her heart rate is down to forty, and she's complaining of breathing discomfort."

He listened with pursed lips. "No wonder," he said. "Have you told Dr. Brayley?"

"Not yet," Mrs. Graham said. "Since she is your patient and you were available, I brought it to your attention first."

The eyes behind Dr. Rodman's glasses were unblinking. "Still, Dr. Brayley did the actual operation."

Mrs. Graham reached for the telephone. "I can call him now."

He raised a pudgy hand in objection. "Wait until I've looked at her myself."

He started down the corridor toward his patient's room, and Mrs. Graham nodded to Edna to accompany him. As she followed the short man's fast pace down the long corridor, Edna recalled that the patient was the young wife of the town's most prosperous car dealer. Her name was Mrs. Walter Short. Edna had gone to school with her and they were on a first name basis.

In a large private room, Mary Short looked up from her pillow with a wan smile. She was a frail, slender blonde girl. She spoke in a weak voice. "I'm sorry to be so much bother, Doctor."

"Not at all," he told her extravagantly. "It is a pleasure to call on so lovely a lady so early in the day." He bent over her, and Edna noted the neat tailored perfection of his dark suit and the large white flower in his buttonhole.

She watched while he fussed over the patient. When he had finished his examination, he gazed at the sick woman with a broad smile on his ugly face. "We will have you feeling better in no time," he assured her.

When they left the room, he glanced worriedly at Edna. "I don't like her condition. I must talk this over with Dr. Brayley."

"Her skin has a soggy, moist condition," Edna volunteered. "Perhaps she is suffering from myxedema."

The squat man glared at her. "An interesting supposition," he said curtly. "Too bad you haven't studied medicine, Nurse."

Edna felt her cheeks crimson at the reproof. She knew that Dr. Rodman was almost insanely touchy and that she should have refrained from any comment.

He stalked ahead of her toward the desk, and she felt almost certain he would make some mention of what she'd said to Mrs. Graham. Whether he would have or not she never discovered, because before they got to the desk her Uncle Charles appeared with a younger man at his side.

Edna guessed that this was the new doctor who had come to assist her uncle. She saw that he was young, with a thoughtful, rather handsome face. He was dark and wore his hair brushed straight back, and he was a few inches taller than her uncle and towered above the squat Dr. Rodman.

Dr. Brayley greeted Dr. Rodman with a smile and introduced him to the newcomer. "This is one of our busiest practitioners," he told the new doctor. "You must expect to see a lot of him."

Dr. Rodman touched the flower in his lapel and importantly appraised the newcomer. "Dr. Preston Halliday," he said, repeating his name. "You have done some papers on the virus theory of cancer."

Dr. Halliday gave a modest smile and nodded. "Some rather unimportant contributions, I'm afraid."

"But all contributions count," Dr. Rodman insisted. He then entered into a long-winded discourse on a number of papers he had prepared on various subjects when in California. "Of course when I came East I dropped them all. But I'll begin again one of these days!"

Edna noted that Dr. Halliday looked slightly embarrassed at this. No doubt he was as skeptical of Rodman's story as was the rest of the hospital.

Dr. Rodman cleared his throat. "By the way, our patient, Mary Short, has breathing difficulties. I think you should look in on her, Dr. Brayley."

"I will," Charles Brayley agreed, "although I think I already have a hint of what the trouble may be."

"Oh, yes?" Dr. Rodman cocked his head at an angle.

"When I saw her yesterday, there were some warning signals," Dr. Brayley went on. "Very often a series of thyroid shots will solve the problem. I'd say she is suffering from myxedema."

The squat man looked startled and glanced at Edna with uneasy eyes. Then he recovered himself and smiled at the hospital head. "My own diagnosis, Dr. Brayley. I'll proceed with the required treatment."

He bowed and stalked off on his rounds. Edna watched him go with a faint smile.

Her uncle took advantage of the opportunity to introduce her to Dr. Halliday. "Not only is she one of our better nurses," he said, "but she also happens to be my niece."

Dr. Preston Halliday gave her one of his quick smiles. "I look forward to having you as a colleague, Miss Brayley."

"I understand you are also going to be my neighbor," she said, returning the smile.

He glanced at her uncle for confirmation. "I haven't been to my apartment yet."

"It's just around the block from Edna's place." Her uncle's eyes twinkled. "And she can cook an excellent roast beef dinner, if you are partial to beef."

Dr. Halliday took the suggestion in good humor. "I must remember that," he said.

"I'm afraid you'll find that my uncle is prejudiced in my favor as regards both my nursing and cooking ability," Edna said, blushing. "But we are happy to have you here."

Edna had a busy afternoon with her patients. She hoped that Bernice wouldn't be too difficult tonight.

When her shift ended, she stepped out into the still bright afternoon sunshine. As she started down the steps, someone called out her name. She turned and saw that it was the new doctor.

Dr. Preston Halliday came down quickly and joined her. "Your uncle saw you leaving," he said, "and thought you might be good enough to show me where I'm to live. The apartment is at 152 Montgomery Avenue."

"Of course," she said. "I'll be glad to. You have a car, I suppose?"

He nodded. "Yes. How about you?"

"I walk to work," she said. "In any case, I don't own a car."

He led her along the gravel walk that fronted the hospital to the parking lot on the town side. "I suppose you hardly need one in a town this size," he said.

"It would come in very handy," she admitted frankly. "But my budget just couldn't afford one."

Dr. Halliday stopped by a modest black sedan. "It does cost money," he agreed, "especially when you consider the taxes and insurance." He unlocked the door and held it open until she got in.

After he was behind the wheel, she gave him some general directions. As they headed out into traffic, she said: "This will be quite a different sort of position for you after your years in research."

He glanced at her with a smile. "That makes me sound ancient. I'm not really."

Edna laughed. "What I mean is, you've spent most of your active professional life in research labs."

He grimaced. "That doesn't sound much better. Actually, I've been in research about five years."

"Most people who stay that long don't leave the field," Edna probed. "You have definitely had a change in interests?"

"Definitely," he said in a grim tone, his eyes straight ahead on the intersection lights that had halted them.

Edna decided she'd better not pursue the matter any further.

A familiar light blue car came abreast of them as they waited for the yellow light to change to green. Edna turned and found herself staring into Jim Boone's surprised face. The light changed, and the cars drew apart as they moved on. But, glancing back, she could still see the shock on Jim's face as he bent over the wheel and knew the situation would require some explaining.

Chapter Three

They drove directly to the building in which Dr. Halliday's apartment was located, and then he insisted on taking her around to her own place. When they finally came to the lovely old dark-shingled house set behind the towering elms, he stared at it with genuine admiration.

"I like it," he said. "You're very fortunate to live in such a restful atmosphere. Not too much of that sort of living available for the majority of us these days."

She found herself looking at the house with new eyes. It did have an other-era quality, and yet the fresh white trim of the porch and windows made it plain that the old building had been lovingly restored. He father had done a good job. She found herself suddenly filled with nostalgia.

"My father was very happy here," she told Preston Halliday. "I'm only sorry he didn't live longer to enjoy it."

"A pity," the young doctor said, and she sensed that he was aware of her sudden mood of sadness and perhaps felt awkward that he'd brought the matter up.

"You must see the inside when you have more time." She smiled at him to put him at his ease.

His solemn face brightened. "I'd enjoy that," he said. "There are so many things I should know about this new city and my new job. I'm sure you can be very valuable to me. I'd like to take you to dinner some time soon so we can have a really good conversation."

"Thank you," she said. "There are some very good places to eat here, especially in the summertime when the resort hotels and shore restaurants are open."

She waited on the sidewalk until she saw that he'd driven off in the right direction. The handsome young doctor had made a good impression on her, even though she sensed there was a certain reserve in his manner.

On her way to the house, she lingered by the rosebushes for a moment to enjoy their fragrant aroma and admire the delicate pink blossoms that had suddenly appeared in profusion. When she finally went inside, she found Bernice standing in the living room. Edna knew at once the blonde woman had been watching her arrival in Dr. Halliday's car.

Bernice eyed her with undisguised curiosity. "That wasn't Jim's car just now," she said.

Edna found herself both amused and annoyed. She said: "No, it wasn't!" and started for the stairway.

Bernice spoke apologetically. "I happened to notice because I've been standing here for ten minutes waiting for a taxi."

Turning, Edna saw that Bernice was dressed to go out. She was wearing a coral summer dress with a string belt of black at the waist. She also had on her pastel mink cape and a tiny white hat perched on the back of her head. There was no question that she looked strikingly beautiful.

Edna said: "It's too bad they've kept you waiting. That was the new doctor's car. He arrived this morning, and Uncle Charles suggested I show him the way up here, since his apartment's near us."

"Oh, yes," Bernice said, pulling on a long white glove. "I remember Charles mentioned that last night." She gave Edna a hurt look. "You might have invited him in. I would have enjoyed meeting him, and perhaps he could have taken me downtown."

Edna sighed. "It didn't seem the proper moment, Bernice. Anyhow, he wouldn't know his way around to drive you anywhere."

Bernice was skeptical. "I don't see why not. It's not that big a place, and I'm going to the Mills estate on the main road. They're having a garden party for the symphony, and afterward I've been invited to the hotel for dinner."

"Wonderful!" Edna told her, genuinely pleased. She knew how much this kind of activity meant to the blonde woman, and she was also happy at the prospect of having the house to herself.

Bernice finished putting on her gloves. "I do manage to have some social life," she said in a sulky tone, "in spite of everything."

Edna said nothing. Just then a car blew its horn in the street, and she glanced out the front door and saw with some relief that the taxi had at last arrived.

"Your taxi is here now," she told Bernice.

The blonde woman brightened and hurried toward the front door. She stopped on the way out to turn and call back: "I won't be late."

Edna smiled. "Don't worry. I'm going out myself. Jim's taking me dancing."

"Oh!" Bernice reverted to her old self immediately. "Well, I must get along!"

The door closed after her, and Edna went up the stairs slowly.

After a bath, she put on a dressing gown, went downstairs again and prepared herself a light salad dinner. As she was finishing a tall glass of iced tea, the phone rang.

It was Jim Boone, and he sounded somewhat worried. "Did I see you in an out-of-state car today?" he asked.

"Yes." She laughed. "I tried to catch your eye but didn't succeed."

There was a pointed pause on the line before Jim said cautiously: "You were with a man, weren't you? A young man?"

"Guilty as charged," Edna told him lightly. "That's the new doctor who's going to assist Uncle Charles at the hospital. I was showing him the way to his apartment."

"Oh!" Jim sounded relieved. "I wasn't quite sure it was you, and I couldn't guess who he might be."

"He's very nice," Edna said. "You must meet him."

"I'll look forward to that," Jim said without much enthusiasm. And then: "Where are we meeting tonight?"

"Pick me up at my place," Edna said smugly.

It was another surprise for Jim. "New deal!" he observed. "I haven't done that in a long while."

"I'm mistress of the house tonight," Edna confided. "Bernice has gone downtown on some social function. You'll be by about eight-thirty?"

"That should make it about right," Jim agreed. "Lots of news to tell you."

After Edna put down the phone, she sat with the evening paper for a while. The blessed quiet of the house was so enjoyable that she put off dressing until the last minute.

Then she hastily selected an interesting rough-woven beige with a full skirt in a pattern of subdued color. It had a belt of rope-like material to give it a carefree peasant touch.

They were going to the Wentworth, one of the largest summer resort hotels in the area, and she felt the dress was suitably chic and yet informal. The hotel had dancing in its Marine Room every week night to a trio brought down from New York. The musicians were much better than the local hands, and so many of the Farmingham residents joined the summer people for the dances. Jim had been quick to discover the place, and it had become one of their favorites.

He arrived a few minutes early, but she managed not to keep him waiting, and they were soon on their way to the hotel. He gave her an admiring glance from behind the wheel. "Someone looks very pretty tonight."

Edna smiled her gratitude demurely. "Someone had a chance to rest after work. It can make a difference."

"I know it," Jim agreed. "By the way, things aren't going to get any easier for you. Dad's checking into the hospital in a couple of days."

Edna laughed. It was hospital gossip that the older Boone was one of the most difficult and tyrannical patients they'd ever treated. His bronchial condition was not severe, but it did threaten to weaken his heart, as the drug manufacturer was overweight.

"Maybe he'll have his same room again," Edna said. "He was on the fourth floor last time, so I didn't see much of him."

"He has it all arranged with your uncle," Jim said. "He thinks the treatment last time helped him a lot. Now he's looking for a complete cure."

Edna nodded. "That seems in character."

"The other big news," Jim told her, "is that Eric is thinking about getting married."

She gave the young man at the wheel a

startled look. "You don't mean it! To the little girl at the playhouse?"

The big blond man nodded. "It's supposed to be kept quiet. I'm the only one he's told. He doesn't want to talk it over with Dad until it's all settled."

"It isn't completely settled then?"

Jim shrugged. "You know what Eric is like. I'm surprised he gave me this much information. Anyway, we'll probably hear more about it before the evening is over. He said he might bring her to the dance after the show."

"She seemed very interesting on stage. I'd like to meet her," Edna said. "What was her name? Nancy —"

"Nancy Carrington," Jim finished for her. "I've met her only a couple of times myself, but there's no question that Eric is badly smitten with her. I've never seen him quite like this before."

They found a parking place near the hotel entrance and made their way into the large, dimly lit dining room, where the central portion of the floor was cleared for dancing. The place was well filled with young couples, even though it was relatively early. The dancing continued until one o'clock.

The *maitre d'*, a plump bald man, advanced to meet them with a broad smile. He knew Jim and was aware that he left big tips. "I have your usual table, Mr. Boone," he said with a slight bow, and led them across the room to a desirable table for two that faced the windows overlooking the ocean.

Already a bright moon was casting a reflection on the water, and as she was helped into chair by the headwaiter, Edna gave him a smiling acknowledgement of her pleasure. "This is nice," she murmured.

"I know it is your favorite spot." The headwaiter smiled benevolently and summoned a waiter to take their order.

Jim looked around the crowded room. "This is really a nice place to spend an evening," he said. Then, smiling at Edna: "What do you natives find to do when these summer spots close?"

"By that time it's too cold to miss them," Edna said. "Speaking for myself, I settle down to a routine of reading and work."

"You should find a job in Boston," Jim suggested. "We could have a lot of fun together. It's a gay town in winter."

"You make it sound very tempting." Edna smiled across the table.

"I'm serious," he said. "You'd have no trouble landing a job in a Boston hospital.

There's nothing to keep you here now. Don't tell me you're so fond of your step-mother you can't consider leaving."

She looked down at the table. "It's more than that. I've spent so many good years here that I think I'd feel lost anywhere else. I hate to think of leaving the house. Dad put so much of himself in it. It's filled with memories of him."

Jim sighed. "Do you think it's right to live with memories?"

"I know it's not healthy," she admitted. "Perhaps I'm developing into a neurotic. I hope not."

"I don't think your father would like the idea," Jim said. "He'd want you to live a full, happy life. You'll never do it as long as you stay in that house."

She looked up at him with a faint smile. "In spite of what you think, I do have a sense of responsibility concerning Bernice. I'd like to know that she's found herself before I make any plans."

"Now you are talking nonsense," Jim said impatiently. "Bernice is quite capable of looking after herself. She's selfish enough to do a fine job of it."

"But she's not always very sensible about what's best for her."

The blond man shook his head with a

hopeless smile. "All right, little mother. Have it your way. The music sounds good. Let's settle this by dancing."

"Best idea you've had," she agreed happily.

The New York band was playing a selection of melodies from the Broadway hit, *Oliver*, and Edna soon found herself lost in the magic of the music. She enjoyed dancing, and Jim made an excellent partner. For a perfect few minutes she forgot all her troubles as they danced in the romantic shadows to the tune of "I'd Do Anything For You" and "As Long As He Needs Me."

When they returned to the table, Jim leaned across and, taking her hand, said solemnly: "You gave me quite a start today. Seeing you in that car with that doctor fellow made me think."

Edna's eyebrows arched in surprise. "Really?"

"To be exact, it made me think about us."

"What about us?"

He lowered his eyes. "We've just been drifting along, Edna, taking each other for granted. I should have gotten around to discussing this a long time ago, but we were getting along so well it didn't seem necessary."

She smiled faintly. "What suddenly makes it so urgent?"

"This afternoon."

"But that's silly!" Edna gave an incredulous little laugh.

"No. Believe me, I'm serious!" Jim raised his eyes to meet hers, and she was surprised to see that there was a troubled expression in them. "I was jealous when I saw you in the car with a strange man. I suddenly realized that I should have told you a long time ago that life wouldn't be much fun for me without you."

Edna spoke with quiet sincerity. "I deeply appreciate that, Jim. But I don't think either of us can really be sure."

He swallowed hard and then said: "What I'm trying to say is that I'm in love with you and I'd like to marry you."

She was stunned by the direct statement. She knew that he was really in earnest, but she was not prepared to answer him at that moment. She said lightly, "I think there must be something in the air. You've definitely caught the romantic bug from Eric!"

"No," he said. "I've thought this out on my own. What do you say?"

She made a pattern with her hand on the tablecloth and kept her eyes on the nervous gesture as she answered: "I'd like to think about it, Jim. We've known each other during the summers. We're not the boy and girl working together in a summer hotel any more. We're grown up now, and what we're thinking about is more than a summer romance between school kids. This is a lifetime thing, or should be, and I don't see that it would work out for us. There are too many differences in our backgrounds."

The blond man sat back with a groan. "Must I always be punished for being a millionaire's son?"

"I'm afraid so." Edna smiled at him with some sadness. "That's one of the differences, but not the most important one, perhaps. I'm basically a small-town girl, and you're a city boy. We get on well together in the summer months when you come down here for a few weeks vacation. But come October, I don't think I'd wear so well. I think you'd tire of me in the city. I wouldn't stand up well against all that debutante competition in the eyes of your family."

"The only family I have that matters is Dad," Jim said, "and he thinks all debutantes are pests! I'll expect an answer before the summer is over," he told her.

"I'll remember," she promised. "And I am flattered."

The blond man looked unhappy. "That sounds more polite than convincing. See that in the meantime you don't accept any other offers."

She gave him a teasing look. "Don't tell me you're worried about Dr. Preston Halliday."

"He's a very handsome hunk of man," Jim grumbled. "Sure I'm worried."

"You needn't be," she said. "Dr. Halliday is interested only in his career."

The orchestra began to play again, and they got up to dance.

Shortly after eleven, when they were seated at their table again, the headwaiter brought over Eric and Nancy. Introductions were made and chairs added to the table. After Eric had ordered, there was a moment of awkward silence.

Edna decided she'd better take the initiative. She smiled at the actress. "We thought you were wonderful in the play the other night."

Nancy seemed to appreciate the compliment. "It's an awfully good part," she said. "I enjoy playing it." She was small, with an alert, intelligent type of beauty.

Edna spoke next to Eric. "You must be very proud of her."

The tall Boone brother's square-cut features wore a sulky expression. "I don't know. I'd just as soon she didn't act at all."

Nancy's bright eyes focused on him with an angry look. "At least now you're telling the truth."

Eric gave the girl a mocking grin. "Why not?"

Jim and Edna exchanged glances. They both sensed that the other two must have had some sort of quarrel on the way to the dance. They both seemed in a tense and unhappy humor, although Nancy Carrington was managing the situation better than the moody Eric.

Jim said: "If you two lovebirds will excuse us, we'd like to dance."

It gave them an excuse to get out on the floor where they could compare notes. Edna looked up at Jim with comic dismay as they danced. "What did you make of all that?"

He lifted his eyebrows. "There's only one answer. They've had a row."

"But I thought this was to be their big night. I even wondered if they might formally announce their engagement."

"You know as much about it as I do." Jim sighed.

"Maybe they'll make up when they're

alone together," Edna suggested. "At least let's hope so!"

But when they returned to the table, the air hadn't cleared. It was plain from the expressions on the faces of Eric and Nancy and from their stilted conversation that they were still angry with each other. Nancy also noticed that Eric had been ordering extra drinks, and his face was now flushed.

He leaned across the table with drunken good humor and said: "How about taking a midnight drive with me, Edna? Let me show you the ocean by moonlight!"

Edna smiled and nodded toward the window. "We have a very good view here."

He waved a hand disgustedly. "No romance in that! You got to see it at top speed to enjoy it. Ride along with your head in the wind!"

Nancy gave him a vicious look. "Your head certainly needs clearing!"

"Good!" He stood up. "Then let's go! We'll give the car a workout!"

"Not me!" Nancy showed alarm as she stared up at him. "You're in no shape to drive."

He wavered above the table uncertainly with a silly smile. "You're trying to make a scene," he accused her.

"No," she said quietly but firmly. "I'm not, Eric. But I won't drive with you as you are now."

Eric turned to Edna again. "How about you?"

Before she could answer, Jim was on his feet and had taken his younger brother by the arm. He spoke to Nancy, saying: "I'll see that you get home, Nancy. You wait here with Edna. We're going out to get some fresh air."

Before a surprised and annoyed Eric could manage any verbal protest, Jim swung him around, and the two headed off in the direction of the entrance. After they'd watched them go, the two girls faced each other.

Nancy said: "I'm sorry about this. I hope we haven't spoiled your evening."

"It's all right," Edna said, "as long as Jim is able to straighten him out. Does this happen often?"

"Pretty often," Nancy said. "I guess he thinks he's entitled to go on a binge tonight."

Edna gave the girl a questioning look. "Why should he?"

"He asked me to marry him, and I refused."

"I see," Edna said quietly. "I suppose he

was upset. He wasn't expecting that sort of answer."

"With the Boone millions to back him up, I suppose it did come as a shock." The redhead shrugged. "Well, I don't want to be the wife of Horace Boone's second son. I want to be somebody on my own. One of these days I'll make my name as an actress."

"That's why you refused him?" Edna said. "Because of your career?"

"Yes." Nancy looked white and forlorn. "He just doesn't seem to understand. I thought he cared enough, but he doesn't."

"You do like him though, don't you?"

Nancy nodded. "Maybe I was in love with him. I don't know. Anyway, it's finished now."

Edna was touched by the girl's unhappiness. She said: "Maybe he'd let you continue your career after you were married."

She shook her head grimly. "Oh, no, nothing as reasonable as that! He won't give an inch!"

Edna looked up and saw a worried Jim coming back across the room to get them. He was alone, so he must have sent Eric on his way. It occurred to her that it hadn't been a very good night romantically for either of the two Boone brothers.

Chapter Four

The next morning when Edna entered the hospital cafeteria, Mel smiled a greeting to her from their usual table. Edna nodded to the blonde nurse, went directly to the counter and filled a tray with her usual breakfast.

Mel's shrewd eyes were bright with excitement as Edna joined her at the table. "Lots of news this morning," the blonde girl said with barely subdued excitement.

Edna sipped her orange juice. "Don't tell me Dr. Rodman has been given a fellowship in the American College of Surgeons."

"That wouldn't be just news." Mel laughed. "I'd have to tag that a disaster."

"Well, you have me nicely hooked with curiosity," Edna said. "I suppose now you're going to let me dangle through toast and coffee."

Mel's almost pretty face shone with delight. "That would come under the heading of mental cruelty," she said. "Did you see Jim last night?"

Edna registered "Yes. Why?"

"Was his brother Eric around?"

She nodded. "As a matter of fact, he joined us for dancing later in the evening. We were at the Wentworth. He brought along Nancy Carrington from the summer theatre."

The blonde nurse gave her a knowing look. "Had he been drinking?"

Edna hesitated before answering.

"Frankly," she said in a reserved tone, "I'd rather not talk about it. It wasn't too pleasant an occasion. Eric did have quite a few drinks."

"You're not giving away any secrets," Mel told her. "Mr. Eric Boone is the morning gossip topic of Farmingham this bright a.m." She leaned forward and went on in a somewhat lower tone: "I stopped by the gas station to fill my car, and they were laughing about it there."

"About what?" Edna found herself asking sharply.

"One of the Elmdale Dairy Trucks found Eric's car in the ditch on the other side of town," Mel said. "Eric was in it, snoring happily behind the wheel. The truck driver woke him up and brought him into Farmingham in the milk truck, and the garage sent a tow truck out to get his car."

Edna was relieved. She stirred her coffee. "Well, I'm glad that's all that's happened."

"It isn't," Mel told her with a mischievous twinkle in her eyes. "Last night Horace Boone drove down late and checked into the hospital. So he's bound to hear all about it. Eric will have some explaining to do before this day is over. His father is pretty tired of his pranks already."

"Well, as long as it doesn't get into the paper," Edna said.

"Not likely, since the police didn't find him." Mel shook her head. "He may be lucky enough to get away with it. I don't suppose I'd have known if I hadn't happened to stop by the garage that sent out the wrecker."

"Have you told anyone else?" Edna asked.

Looking slightly guilty, Mel said: "No, not yet."

Edna raised her eyes to meet those of her friend. "Do you think it's worth repeating?"

Mel's cheeks colored. "I suppose not."

Edna smiled. "If Horace Boone gets the news and becomes really upset, we'll all suffer on the third floor. He's difficult enough when he's in a good humor."

The tension between them eased, and

Mel laughed. "In the interests of the third, I'll cradle my juicy bit of scandal close to me." The tall girl got up with a wink. "But it won't be easy!"

Left alone to finish her coffee, Edna thought about their conversation.

Her reverie was interrupted by a male voice at her shoulder saying: "Good morning, Miss Brayley."

She turned to look up into the handsome, smiling face of Dr. Preston Halliday. She said: "I didn't see you when I came in. You've decided to become one of the morning regulars at the cafeteria?"

He nodded. "It seems a sensible arrangement for a bachelor. I found myself a quiet corner where I could read with my coffee."

Edna laughed. "*The Medical Journal?*"

He held up a pocket-sized magazine with a red cover and the figure of a man drawn in straight black lines with a small halo above his head. "Nothing so erudite," he told her. "It's the *Saint Magazine*. I like Leslie Charteris' mystery yarns."

At least we haven't another poseur like Dr. Rodman, Edna thought thankfully. She said: "It's a sign of brains to enjoy good detective fiction."

"I'm afraid I'll have to prove I have

brains a much harder way," he told her wryly. "I'm on my way now to start straightening out my office." With a warm nod of farewell, he went on out to the corridor.

A few minutes later, Edna took the elevator up to the third floor and began the routine duties of the day. She noted that Horace Boone had already been seen by one of the other nurses and was grateful for this. The big man could be a problem on a busy morning.

She finished with Bill Griffin, her uncle's gastrectomy patient, who was showing definite signs of improvement. He gave her a wry smile. "The only bad part about getting well," he said, "is that I'll have to give up this quiet room and all the good service."

Edna smiled down at him. "We seldom get such compliments. You'll feel differently in a few days. Most of our patients are anxious to be on their way home before they are ready."

The thin man shook his head. "Not me, Nurse." Back at the desk, she told Head Nurse Emma Graham what her patient had said. The older woman gave her a bleak look from behind her horn-rimmed glasses.

She said: "I can understand his feelings. Bill's a hard worker. He's been in Bradmore's Auto Body Repair Shop for years. Listens to that clamor all day and then goes home to a nagging wife. No wonder his ulcer just came up and burst! What he needs at home is less cold shoulder and warm tongue."

Edna knew that Emma Graham was right. Back of many of their patients' illnesses were psychological causes.

When she made her first morning visit to the New York columnist, David Danton, she found him up and reading. He glanced away from his paper and greeted her with a cheery smile. Edna noticed that he had shaved and so looked less ill than he had on the previous day.

She said: "We're very handsome this morning. Miraculous what a razor can do for a male."

The columnist smiled faintly. "Another day's growth of beard and I'd have frightened you out of the room. Anyway, I do feel better this morning."

"There you are," she said, checking his chart. "Just being here has made you feel better."

"I won't agree with that," he said. "But at least I've decided I'm in good hands."

She took his temperature and noted it down. "You should have some word about your X-rays soon?"

He nodded. "Dr. Brayley has promised a report this morning."

"Well, then you'll know."

His face clouded with worry. "Yes," he said quietly, "then I'll know."

She saw that he was badly worried and knew that there was no point in trying foolishly to minimize his fears. He was much too sensitive and intelligent to accept any routine professional bluffing. That was his trouble: his nervous, sensitive nature made him a poor patient.

When she returned to the desk, Head Nurse Emma Graham had the phone in her hand, waiting for a call. She placed a palm against the mouthpiece and spoke frantically to Edna. "Would you please go down to Mr. Boone's room and see what the trouble is. His light went on a few minutes ago, and there's been no one handy."

Edna nodded and hurried down the corridor with some misgivings. She had had only a very little to do with Horace Boone on his previous visit, and it had been enough. He was hardly ever in a good temper.

When she entered his room, the big man

glared at her from his bed. "About time somebody answered. What do you do around here? Let your patients die waiting?" He was comfortably banked up against a stack of pillows, and the features of his face were blurred by fat. The effect of a pink, featureless balloon poised on a stout body was emphasized by the almost completely bald head with its wispy fringe of white hair.

She said: "I'm sorry, Mr. Boone. Everyone was busy."

"Busy doing nothing!" he said petulantly. He spoke in the hoarse, rasping wheeze of the true asthmatic.

"Can I help you?" she asked.

He glared at her with his porcine blue eyes. "Look at that window!" He pointed to it with a fat hand.

She looked at it for a moment without grasping his meaning. Then she saw that the sun had moved its position so that it was streaming in on the fat man. "I'll adjust the blinds," she said, and went over to do it.

From his propped-up position, Horace Boone continued to complain. "A man could be blinded for all they care! I'm going to talk to Dr. Brayley about this."

It seemed to Edna that it would have not

been too great a task for the drug king to have looked after the blinds himself. He was a walking patient, and he would merely be giving himself some badly needed exercise by stirring from the bed and taking care of the problem.

She came back to his bedside. "That's better, isn't it?"

He regarded her sourly. "It will do. The room's overheated now."

"I'll put the window up a little," she said.

As she did so, he started another line of questioning in his wheezing tone. "Why hasn't the doctor been to see me? I haven't any time to waste in here. Where is Dr. Rodman?"

Edna might have guessed that the rich Horace Boone would be one of the ugly little doctor's patients. Rodman specialized in wealthy neurotics. She said: "He should be making his rounds within the hour."

"Not very businesslike," the fat millionaire observed. "I'd never have built a business with hours like his."

"He visits the patients on the lower floors first. I'm sure he's down there now," she informed the big man politely.

Horace Boone's chin rippled with indignation. "Then have Mrs. Graham phone him down there and tell him I'm waiting."

"I'll tell her, sir," Edna said, and took the opportunity to hurry out of the room.

Back at the desk, she gave his message to Emma Graham. The head nurse merely made a grimace. "He can wait his turn," she said. "You had a call from downstairs. Your uncle wants to see you in his office."

"Is it urgent?" Edna asked, reluctant to leave the busy floor.

"When ever your uncle calls, you can be sure it is." Emma Graham's eyes were solemn behind the horn-rimmed glasses. "You'd better go right down."

Edna took the elevator and then made the short walk down the corridor to the superintendent's office. On the way, she passed the office that Dr. Preston Halliday had taken over and saw him at his desk in earnest conversation with one of the young women from the secretarial staff. He didn't notice her go by.

The door to her uncle's office was open, and she went in. He looked up from the work on his desk and indicated the door with his hand. "Close that, will you please, Edna? And sit down."

She seated herself across from him and saw that his face wore a troubled expression.

He folded his hands on the desk and, clearing his throat, leaned forward. "I've gotten the plates on David Danton," he said in a grave voice. "They are not good."

"Oh!" she said.

"I wanted to talk to you about them before I go upstairs," her uncle continued. "You've been seeing him a good deal. What would you say his present state of mind is?"

"He's feeling better this morning," she said. "But he's not very happy in the hospital."

Her uncle's eyes studied her from behind his glasses. He spoke with great precision. "Would you say that he is frightened, badly frightened?"

She paused and then with a sigh admitted it. "Yes, I suppose he is."

"I've felt that from the first." Her uncle lowered his eyes to the desk. "I noticed it when I first examined him. I could tell by his strained breathing and the way he perspired. It was more than his condition of weakness. What I saw in him was plain fear."

"You think he is very ill?"

"I know it now that I've studied his plates." Her uncle raised his eyes to hers. "There's a main growth pressing against the esophagus, and some other smaller ones, near the glands in his chest and the area of the nerves controlling the larynx. I'm surprised his vocal chords haven't been involved."

She hesitated. "You think it's a malignancy?"

"The chances are very great that it is." He sighed.

"Then you'll have to operate at once?"

"Danton will require an immediate operation," her uncle agreed. He passed a hand wearily across his forehead. "I wish that he'd go back to New York, let some specialist there take on the surgery."

Edna glanced at her hands. "I doubt that he'll agree."

"I know." Her uncle got up and began to pace up and down beside his desk. "He's afraid now, and I don't want to frighten him any worse. But he has to be told that he requires surgery. And I'll have to advise that he see a specialist."

"Perhaps his wife may be able to help," Edna suggested.

Dr. Brayley shook his head as he continued pacing. "I think not. I talked to her on the phone a short time ago. She seemed very scatterbrained. Charming, but very definitely the vague type. I don't see any help there."

"Is there anything you want me to do, to say?"

He stopped his pacing and stood before her. "No. I wanted to let you know the situation and get your opinion of his mental state. I'll be going up to tell him in a few minutes, and I'll need you to help me with my examination."

Back on the third floor, she whispered to Head Nurse Graham that David Danton's X-rays had proven he was in a serious condition. The middle-aged nurse nodded soberly.

"I'm not surprised," she said. "Be careful not to discuss it with any of the others. He couldn't stand it if news like that got back to him."

Edna knew what the senior nurse meant. It took a surprisingly short time for the staff grapevine to spread any bad news about a patient around the hospital.

When her uncle came up to see David Danton, he had her go into the room with him. Danton stood at their entrance, a faint, expectant smile on his face. "It's a lovely day, Doctor," he said. "Tell me I can go home."

Charles Brayley met this with a patient

smile. "I must do that, but not today." He motioned the columnist to the easy chair. "Sit down."

"You've read my plates, Doctor," David Danton said anxiously.

Charles Brayley nodded brusquely. "Yes. We can discuss them later. First I'd like to make a short check to verify a few things. Take off your pajama coat, please."

Edna took the pajama top as the columnist unbuttoned it and slipped it off. She was struck by the emaciated condition of his body. She had no idea that he'd gotten so thin.

Her uncle began his examination. It followed the usual procedure in such cases. He went over David Danton's chest area and shoulders, using his trained, slender fingers and chatting casually as he worked to put the patient at ease.

"I suppose you do a certain number of your daily columns ahead," he said as he used palpation to determine the consistency of certain areas, alert to whether a region was hard or soft, to the temperature and humidity of the skin.

The columnist winced as the pressing fingers found a tender spot. "That seems sore," he observed hastily. And then: "Yes. I keep about three weeks ahead. I also phone anything that is a special break into New York and have it added to that day's column."

"I see," Dr. Brayley said. "Then you could take that long a time off?"

"I could manage a month if I knew ahead," David Danton said. "I have an excellent assistant who collects rough drafts of material for my selection. That helps."

"It should," Dr. Brayley said with an interest that seemed genuine. "How many papers do you service?"

"I have a hundred and twenty-four now. We used to have close to a hundred and fifty, but one chain left us."

"I suppose that happens," Dr. Brayley murmured, skillfully going on with his examination. He was using direct auscultation now as he placed his ear to the columnist's chest and listened for a few seconds. Raising his head, he asked: "Do you ever have any trouble with your throat?"

David Danton looked at him in surprise. "Now that you mention it, I have had some hoarseness and phlegm lately. It must be some sort of allergy. There are a lot of them around in these areas in summer, aren't there?"

The doctor nodded agreement. "They're

very common. You can put on your jacket again."

As Edna helped David Danton into the pajama top, she let her eyes meet her uncle's and knew that the throat symptoms the columnist had just complained about had nothing to do with allergies.

Now her uncle relaxed on the bed and smiled at his patient. "I don't want you to be upset," he said. "There's nothing to worry about as yet. But you do have a blockage that must be removed before you'll enjoy any more normal meals."

David Danton looked at him with appealing eyes. "I need an operation?"

"The sooner the better. I want to see you well again," Charles Brayley said. "Perhaps it would be wise to have it done in New York, where you'll be closer to your work in case you're convalescent longer than expected."

There was a moment of silence. Then David Danton shook his head. "No, Doctor. Whatever has to be done I want done here, and by you."

Charles Brayley sighed. "Please consider what I've said carefully."

The columnist looked straight at him. "I have faith in you, Doctor."

"Thank you," her uncle said quietly.

Chapter Five

Later, when Edna was at the desk, little Dr. Rodman strutted up to her with a smile on his ugly face. "You made a very pretty picture at the dance last night, Nurse Brayley," he said in his smooth manner.

She raised her eyebrows. "I didn't see you there."

He stood with his head thrown back and raised a hand theatrically. "Ah, but I was among those present. My wife and I came with a party about ten. We didn't stay more than an hour."

"It's a very good orchestra." Edna smiled. "I'll be sorry to see it go."

He nodded sagely. "Yes, we do not have too much activity in the winter. Of course I have my chess, but I miss the gay life." The little man sighed. "I used to waltz the nights away in California. I have Austrian blood, you know."

"How interesting," she murmured, trying hard not to smile. At one time or another Dr. Rodman had laid claim to a blood line in nearly every European country.

He shrugged in his affected way. "Well, all my friends have left the coast. I'm probably not missing much. It is good to be here in Maine, even if one's talents are not fully recognized."

"How is your patient, Mr. Boone?" she asked, changing the subject.

Dr. Rodman suddenly looked forlorn. He peered around surreptitiously and then, sure no one else was within hearing distance, said in a loud theatrical whisper: "He is a boor and a nuisance!"

Just then Emma Graham came back and regarded them with an interested glance. Dr. Rodman, as though suddenly frightened, quickly went off in the direction of the elevator. The head nurse chuckled.

"What were you two plotting with your heads together?" she asked Edna.

"Our California medicine man is in one of his down moods," Edna said with a smile. "I think Horace Boone is a bit too much for him."

Emma Graham shook her white-capped head with a weary sigh. "He's too much for all of us. Did you hear him complain about the food at noon?"

"I heard some strange bellowing noises down the hall," Edna said.

"That was our hero," the head nurse said

grimly. "Believe me, sometimes I wonder if it's worth it. Once I get this last boy through college, I won't be here listening to these sad tunes."

Edna patted her on the arm. "You'd be lost without all this, and you know it."

About mid-afternoon Dr. Charles Brayley came back to see David Danton and brought Dr. Halliday with him. They spent some time in the room with the columnist, but she did not notice when they left.

It was close to three and the end of her shift when a rather striking woman of about forty emerged from the elevator. She had a round, pleasant face, brown hair touched with gray and a prominent mouthful of large but perfect teeth that revealed themselves when she smiled.

She came directly to Edna. "I'm Mrs. David Danton," she introduced herself. "How is my husband this afternoon?"

"He seemed to be feeling better when I saw him last," Edna said.

The woman stared at her and continued to smile. "I'm sure you must be the nurse he told me about. Dark and pretty seems to fit you neatly."

Edna blushed. "Your husband is a model patient. He mentioned that he wanted us to meet."

They walked down to the columnist's room and went in together. He was seated in the chair, calmly reading his usual book. Seeing them, he put it down, got up and came over and kissed his wife. Then he smiled at Edna. "So you two finally have gotten together."

"I recognized her at once," Mrs. Danton gushed, giving Edna an admiring look.

She led her husband back to his armchair and cooed: "Now you must sit down and rest. We don't want you overdoing things."

The columnist glanced back at Edna with a bemused look. "I'm not all that sick, darling," he assured his wife. "Ask Miss Brayley. She'll tell you I get around pretty well. I even take a stroll in the corridor now and then."

Edna smiled. "The doctors recommend limited exercise whenever possible."

"Well, isn't that nice!" Mrs. Danton revealed all her pearly teeth in another simpering smile.

David Danton spoke from his chair, a sad smile on the gaunt features. "The doctors were both in this afternoon. They've come to a decision. They're going to operate on me on Monday morning. Dr. Brayley will operate and Dr. Halliday will assist."

Mrs. Danton raised a hand to her bosom. She stared at her husband. "Operate? Isn't this a sudden decision?"

"Somewhat," he admitted. "But from what they've told me, the X-ray plates made it clear I require immediate surgery."

His wife sat down heavily on the bed and threw a despairing glance in Edna's direction. "Isn't this nice news to greet me with!"

Edna said lightly: "I'm sure Dr. Brayley will take no risks."

Mrs. Danton touched a small hankie to her eyes. "You never know what will happen," she sniffed. She turned to her husband. "Did they say it was cancer?"

Edna saw him stiffen at the dread word, but his face put on a mask of calm. "That wasn't mentioned. They can't know the nature of my trouble until they operate."

Edna was angry at the woman for her tactlessness. But at the same time she knew that there was no intentional cruelty in what she'd said. Mrs. Danton simply wasn't too bright.

"I'm sure you needn't upset yourself about Mr. Danton," she told the woman on the bed. "I think he's very wise to face up to his problem and go ahead with what has to be done."

David Danton gave her a grateful smile. "Now you're making me sound like a hero. I'm far from that."

"No one is a hero to his valet or his nurse," Edna joked. "That's not the exact quotation, but it is near enough. Now, if you'll excuse me —"

As she was leaving the hospital, she met Dr. Halliday in the lobby. He stopped and said: "I was hoping you hadn't left yet."

"Really?" she said. "Why?"

"I'd like to have you accept that invitation for dinner tonight," he said. "I understand the summer hotel here serves very fine food. The Wentworth, isn't it?"

She smiled. "It is very good. But are you sure this is a good night for you? You've only just arrived."

"I'd like very much to make it tonight," he said. "Remember, I'm depending on you to help fill in my background on things local."

"Very well," she agreed. "You know where to find me."

"I think I'll be able to retrace my steps," he said with a smile. "How about seven?"

"I'll be ready," she promised.

When she arrived home, she discovered Bernice sprawled out on the divan, listening to the hi-fi set.

Edna studied her white working shoes. "I hope you don't mind having dinner alone tonight."

"I do mind!" Bernice said sharply, sitting up with a troubled look. "What are you going to do?"

"I've been invited out to dinner," Edna said, "by the new doctor."

"Oh!" Bernice looked and sounded completely miserable. "Too bad he didn't invite me as well. But then three is a crowd."

"That's what they say," Edna agreed, getting up and starting for the stairway. She hesitated with her hand on the banister. "I'll cook you a steak before I leave, and have some tomato juice with you. He's not coming until seven."

"Don't go to a lot of bother," Bernice protested faintly.

"It's no bother," Edna assured her.

In her room, she threw herself on the bed for a few minutes before taking a quick shower.

Later, when she came down in her housecoat to press the burgundy dress she intended to wear, she found Bernice flitting around the living room with a dustcloth in hand. The blonde woman stopped and looked up when she realized Edna was standing staring at her.

She made a wry face. "The place is filthy. I thought I'd get rid of some of the dust before your company arrived."

"It can't be so bad," Edna said firmly. "I cleaned it last weekend."

Bernice went back to her dusting. "We're so near the street that dirt collects fast."

Bernice's symptoms and excitement were familiar. Edna gave a sigh, went out to the kitchen and gave her dress a quick pressing. By the time she had finished, it was six-thirty. Still in her dressing gown, she sat at the kitchen table to drink her tomato juice with Bernice.

Just then the object of her concern came into the room in one of her most elaborate dresses. It was white with gold thread woven in a pattern through it, and the flowing skirt had several golden stripes at the bottom. Her blonde hair was neatly done up, and she had on long earrings. There was a strong odor of perfume floating about her as she stood before the astounded Edna with one of her most innocent smiles.

"I dressed so I could answer the door," she said sweetly: "I knew you'd need some extra time to get ready."

Edna had to smile. "You're looking pretty grand for a door-opener!"

Bernice glanced at her dress disparagingly and said: "It's one of my oldest!" Then she carefully arranged the skirt and sat down to drink her tomato juice.

Edna was on the way downstairs when the front doorbell rang. She had hurried into her clothes to be ready on time. Bernice must have been poised, waiting. She was at the door even before the bell stopped ringing.

She welcomed the nonplussed Preston Halliday with a gay: "Of course you're Dr. Halliday! Edna's told me all about you! I'm her stepmother."

By the time Edna got down, Bernice had already ushered the doctor into the living room and seated him in a chair. She took the one closest to it, and Edna had a suspicion she must have arranged them when she was dusting.

Bernice smiled coyly at the somewhat uneasy Preston Halliday and said: "You mustn't get the wrong idea. I married very young, and my late husband was much older. So although I'm Edna's stepmother, I'm actually almost her own age. It's really quite fantastic!"

Edna stepped into the room, determined to rescue the young doctor. "I hope I haven't kept you waiting," she said.

He got up at once, looking relieved to see her. "Not really," he said, glancing at his watch. "I'm actually a few minutes early."

"Well, we can go now," Edna said, taking a step toward the door. "You can leave the porch light on, Bernice."

"I'll do that," Bernice said in her brightest tone as she also reluctantly got up. "It's too bad you have to go, Doctor, just when we were getting to know one another. We must have you here to dinner sometime."

"Thank you." He bowed and started uncertainly after Edna.

Bernice followed him. "I'll be seeing you at the hospital. I'm a volunteer worker there, you know."

"Most admirable," Dr. Halliday smiled over his shoulder. "I hope we meet again. Good night."

Bernice stood on the porch waving after them in a gay, quite unnecessary way until they drove out of sight. Edna sat back against the seat with a sigh of relief. She said: "In case you didn't notice, my stepmother is the eager type."

He laughed. "She is quite imposing."

"She's not a bad sort if you like her sort," Edna assured him. "My father seemed very happy with her, although he died soon after they were married. For his sake, I try to get along."

"I'm sure you do very well," he remarked.

"It's just that she gets a lot of romantic notions," Edna said, "and when they go sour, as they almost always do, she collapses on my hands in a complaining heap."

"That could be a problem."

"Believe me, it is," she assured him. "But maybe one day another Mr. Right will come along, and Bernice's world will brighten permanently."

He gave her a friendly glance. "I sincerely hope so," he said, "for both your sakes."

The same headwaiter showed them to a table, and if he recognized Edna from the previous night, he was suitably discreet and concealed it. The dinner proved excellent, and afterwards they stayed on for conversation and dancing.

Dr. Preston Halliday was a charming companion. Their conversation was mostly about the hospital. Edna mentioned David Danton.

Preston Halliday's face clouded. "Poor fellow," he said. "It isn't going to be easy for him."

"I know," she agreed quietly. "Uncle Charles almost told me he thought the growth was malignant."

"There's small doubt of it," Halliday said. "I think metastasis is already present."

"Then there is nothing you can do?"

"Nothing."

"Poor Mr. Danton," she said. "I hope you're wrong. I think he has an idea that it's cancer. He's been very frightened. Today he surprised me. He took the news of the operation very well."

Preston Halliday opened his palms. "In all of us there are unexpected resources. When the time comes, there is often surprising strength."

She nodded. "I suppose this will be your first operation in a long while."

"Yes," he said. I will only be assisting your uncle. It seems strange to picture myself as a surgeon again."

She looked at him very directly. "You were so dedicated to research, why did you ever leave it?"

He stared at her in faint surprise. "I didn't expect you to ask that question."

"And I suppose I should hardly expect an answer?"

"I don't know that I have one," he said.

He looked at the dancing couples and then, after a moment, turned to her again. "All that I can tell you is that it lost its appeal for me. Quite frankly, I'm what you might call disillusioned."

"Why? Isn't research the most important branch of medicine? Hasn't it given us most of the advances we have now? Isn't it the hope of the future?" She posed the questions one after another and then waited for his answer.

He smiled. "I used to endorse all those views. I suppose I still do. But I found many of my co-workers in the field a little short of dedicated. Many of them are narrow-minded and selfishly ambitious. Twice I had important findings discarded because my seniors were playing lab politics. The second time finished me. I resigned from the labor and from the research field as well."

"I see." She studied him intently. "I knew there was a hint of mystery about you. So it's just frustration."

"All right," he said, "I'm bitter. I think I have a right to be."

"So you've thrown all that accumulated knowledge away for a routine job here at the hospital."

"Maybe I can do more good in a routine

job," he said simply.

"You'll be valuable to us," she agreed. "I won't deny that. But if you live long enough with this bitterness, if you surrender to it completely, then I'm sure your value will decrease even for us."

He looked at her with serious eyes. "You're a remarkable woman," he said.

She shook her head. "I'm just playing big sister. But I do think it's true. Bitter, frustrated people never give of their best to others. In your profession, that could be a tragedy."

"I am a dedicated doctor, if that's what's worrying you," he said. "But don't expect me to rush off to the nearest lab."

They danced until almost eleven, and then he drove her home. The porch light was on, as Bernice had promised, and the living room light as well. Edna had an idea that her stepmother was there waiting, in the hope that Preston Halliday would come in again. For that reason alone she had no intention of inviting him in. It had been a wonderful evening, and she had no intention of spoiling it.

The young doctor sat back from the wheel. "This has been good for me," he said.

She eyed him teasingly. "The food or the company?"

He laughed. "Both. But especially the company. I expected Charles Brayley to have a lovely niece, but you surpassed my expectations."

"You'll do fine in general practice," she assured him. "You have the best of bedside manners."

"Better than your Dr. Rodman?"

Edna laughed. "Well, you haven't his pompous manner, and you lack a flower in the buttonhole."

"Those I can acquire," he assured her. And then soberly: "I am glad that I decided to come to Farmingham."

"So am I," she said sincerely.

Chapter Six

Saturday morning brought a drastic end to the fine weather. When Edna woke up, the first thing she heard was the heavy rain beating against the windows of her room. The walk to the hospital was not really long, but she didn't look forward to it, and on a wet morning like this there would be no chance of getting a taxi.

By the time she had dressed and gone downstairs, the storm seemed to have increased. She quickly donned her plastic raincoat and hood and debated whether or not to try using her umbrella. The wind seemed high, and it might be more of a nuisance than a help. Also, she'd had one umbrella turned completely inside out and ruined by a strong coastal wind such as there was now. She wished that she could ignore her budget and buy herself a small used car.

As she stood in the hallway, the phone rang. It was Mel Parker.

"I hoped I'd catch you home," Mel said. "I'll pick you up and save you from being drowned."

She was glad to accept the invitation. "I've just been standing here in the hallway trying to raise my courage enough to start out."

"I'll be right by," Mel promised. "I'm leaving now."

Edna went out to the porch and waited under its shelter until Mel's car appeared. Then she ran out and got into it. She sat back on the seat with a laugh and a gasp. "I'm drenched even in that short distance," she said.

Mel's eyes were fastened on the street ahead. "These windshield wipers don't seem to clean the windshield," she complained. "They must be worn or badly adjusted."

Edna looked out at the torrential rain. "I think it's mostly because the rain is coming down so heavily."

"Maybe so," Mel agreed, still peering nervously through the rain-distorted glass. "I was out to the summer theatre last night."

"Good," she said. "Did you like it?"

"I had a lot of fun," Mel said. "That little Nancy Carrington, the redhead, is clever. I'll bet she turns up on Broadway some day."

"I wouldn't be surprised," Edna said.

"She seems very determined about her career."

Mel was occupied for a moment as she wheeled the car through a busy intersection and into the traffic of the main business street. When they were in the regular line of cars again, she relaxed and glanced at Edna with a grin. "Eric Boone was there as usual."

Edna smiled. "I'm not surprised. He's very interested in the playhouse."

"You mean he's very interested in Nancy Carrington. Everyone around town is talking about it."

"Well, it makes a good summer topic." Edna shrugged. "And Eric has to keep himself in the public eye one way or another."

"I don't suppose it's as dangerous a hobby as smashing up sports cars as he has been doing." Mel laughed. "Or maybe it's more dangerous."

"I suppose that depends on how seriously they both take it."

"When Eric buys a seat for the theatre every night in the week, I'd say he's as serious as he can get."

Edna was doubtful. "I don't know. It's a novelty, and he enjoys shocking the locals. Most of them think they are doing well if they show up at the theatre once or twice a season. Naturally, his being there every night impresses them. And that's exactly what Eric wants."

"What does Jim think of it?" Mel asked slyly.

"You know what brothers are like. He knows Eric has been seeing this girl, but he hasn't said much about it. Jim is pretty self-centered."

"The boys are pretty good when you consider the mighty Horace," the blonde girl said. "Has Jim got a touch of his father's disposition?"

"He's pretty definite in his opinions," Edna replied as she stared out at the passing vista of the rainy street. "But he hasn't reached the ranting stage. Maybe when he gets older, he will."

"That's a sweet thought!" Mel sighed.

Edna looked at her with a smile. "I had a very nice evening last night. Dr. Halliday took me out to dinner."

Mel shot her an astonished glance. "Well, you don't lose much time!"

"It was his idea."

"Then *he's* a fast worker," the blonde nurse said. "Do you like him?"

"Very much," Edna said. "I was able to fill him in on a lot of our local picture.

That was the main purpose of our getting together."

The blonde nurse swung her car into a parking space on the hospital lot with a scattering of gravel and braked it to a jolting halt. She eyed Edna with amusement. "Don't expect me to believe that!"

"But it's true!" Edna insisted.

Mel shook her head. "At this rate, you won't have to wait until Jim gets older to reach the ranting stage. Wait until he finds out about Preston Halliday!"

They dodged out into the rain and ran quickly up the hospital steps. When they went to the cafeteria for breakfast, Edna looked around to see if there was any sign of the young doctor, but he wasn't there. She decided he'd probably arrived earlier, had his breakfast and gone up to his office.

There were several patients being discharged on the third floor, and this meant extra paper work for Head Nurse Emma Graham. She glanced up from her desk with a perplexed look when Edna reported for duty.

"Seems I spend more time filling in forms than I do nursing these days," she complained. "Nearly every patient we get has some kind of insurance. I'm getting to know more about the different companies and their claim forms than I do about taking care of sick people."

Edna laughed. "Cheer up. One of these days they'll install a neat little automatic machine here that will take care of all that. Then you'll get back to nursing."

Emma Graham bent over her paper-strewn desk. "I can hardly wait for automation," she said sourly.

Edna went about the usual morning duties. After she'd finished with the patient recovering from the gastrectomy, she went on to David Danton's room. He surprised her by still being in bed.

Noticing her expression, he laughed. "I'm treating myself. I've always liked to stay in bed late on rainy days. It's the only way I can relax."

She readied the thermometer. "I'm so happy you're doing it," she said, genuinely pleased.

When she had finished with him, he said: "I'm glad you met my wife."

"Yes," Edna agreed. "It was lucky she came when she did. A few minutes later and I'd have been off duty."

There was a pause, and she had the feeling he was waiting for her to say something more about the meeting. She found herself unable to go on. She hadn't been impressed with his wife, and she respected him too much to lie to him. It was an awkward moment.

Perhaps the columnist sensed what she was thinking, for he changed the subject. "I'm actually looking forward to my operation," he said. "It will be great to tackle a good slice of sirloin again."

"I know," she agreed. "It must be dreadful not to be able to take anything but liquids."

"It's better than choking to death." David Danton looked grim. "That's what almost happened to me the last time I tried to eat a steak."

"Well, now you'll clear that problem up," she said.

"I'm desperate enough to try anything." He smoothed his thin hands across the bed covering in a nervous motion. "Of course my wife takes a pretty dim view of the entire business."

"I don't think she understands," Edna suggested. "And she's frightened for you."

He sighed. "I suppose that's it." He raised his eyes to meet hers. "She seems to be obsessed with the idea that I have cancer. Is that what everyone thinks, what they are all saying behind my back?"

Edna shook her head. "Whatever gave you that idea?"

The columnist shrugged. "Sitting here alone, you get all sorts of ideas. I know it could be cancer. I just hope it isn't."

"No one can tell you anything about the obstruction until after your operation," Edna said seriously. "Guesses don't count in a case like this."

"How soon will they know?" he asked. "I mean, how soon after they operate?"

"They'll send a specimen to the lab directly from the O.R.," Edna explained. "They might have a report back late in the afternoon; by the next morning, anyway."

"I see," the columnist said thoughtfully.

"Of course Dr. Brayley will have some idea at once," she said. "But the final verdict must come from the lab."

"I imagine Monday morning will be pretty hard for my wife," Danton said slowly. "She'll want to come here and visit a few minutes before it begins."

Edna nodded. "She can come in early."

"And Dr. Brayley will be able to give her some immediate word when it's over?" he asked.

She smiled. "That's the usual procedure. There's no reason your wife couldn't wait here in your room while the operation is going on. Then Dr. Brayley will know exactly where to find her, and he can come up for a few minutes when he's finished."

David Danton brightened. "That sounds very nice," he said. "I want to make it as easy for her as I can."

"Of course," she said. Then, going to the door: "Now you enjoy this lovely rain and don't keep thinking about Monday. Let Dr. Brayley worry about that. It's his responsibility."

The columnist chuckled. "Yes, but don't forget it's my neck!"

She left him in what she hoped was a better state of mind.

Two of the rooms on floor three were now empty, and it was likely that they would remain so over the weekend. It was rarely that patients were entered on Saturday unless they were in the emergency class. Mel paused in the corridor to speak to Edna a moment. The blonde nurse sighed. "Maybe things are going to ease a bit here."

It seemed that she had no sooner said the words before Head Nurse Emma Graham came hurrying down to them. Edna took one glance at the older nurse's face and knew that something unexpected had happened.

Emma Graham seemed breathless and excited. "Have another bed put in 306. We're making it into a semi-private. And we'll have a patient for 310 as well. A car skidded into a pole on the main highway. Three women were in it. The ambulance is bringing them here now."

Within a few minutes an orderly was placing an extra bed in 306, and they were making ready for the arrival of the accident victims. A Mrs. Barlow had been the driver of the car, Edna learned later; she was an elderly, wealthy widow and one of Dr. Rodman's patients.

When the ambulance brought in the three women, it turned out that Mrs. Barlow was more seriously injured than her companions, who were also in the older age group. Her ribs had been crushed on one side, and she had a leg broken in two places. Dr. Brayley hurried her to the operating room and administered a mild anesthetic to enable him to take care of the damaged ribs and set the injured leg. She was suffering from shock and seemed hardly aware of what was taking place when she was transferred to the O.R.

Meanwhile, Dr. Halliday was taking care of the other two women in the treatment room. They were also suffering from shock, and one of them, a thin, rather frail woman, had a bad cut on her forehead which required some stitches. The other woman seemed to have no specific injuries other than bruises and minor cuts. She was a dumpy little creature who moaned continually. Once she had been given a sedative, she quieted down and seemed in the best condition of the three.

These two patients were soon transferred to room 306, and Dr. Halliday, who had come upstairs with them, warned Edna: "I think we've taken care of all their troubles. But keep a sharp eye on them. There's always the chance of some internal injury or even an unsuspected head injury. Let me know if they complain of any suspicious symptoms."

She was impressed by the efficient, thorough way in which he handled the case.

Shortly after this, her uncle brought up the most seriously injured woman. She was installed in 310, and Mel was assigned to look after her. Dr. Brayley paused at the desk to give Emma Graham a sympathetic smile. "Blame it on the rain, Emma," he said. "You're having a busy weekend after all."

She shook her head. "At least tomorrow

is my day off," she said. "And Dr. Rodman phoned. He's on his way here now to see Mrs. Barlow."

Dr. Brayley nodded. "I think we've done about all we can for her."

When the squat, ugly little doctor arrived, he checked Mrs. Barlow's chart and went inside to see her. When he emerged, he came back to the desk with his usual manner of fussy importance.

"We must get a private nurse for Mrs. Barlow," he said emphatically. "I know that is what she would want me to do."

Emma Graham looked doubtful. "Do you think she really needs one, Doctor?"

Dr. Rodman opened his eyes wide. "I want her to have a private duty nurse. I don't think we have to discuss it."

It was an indirect reproval of the head nurse, and he seemed not to care that Edna was standing near the desk and within easy hearing distance.

Emma Graham's face reddened. "I'll try, Doctor," she said. "They are not easy to get. So many are away on vacation."

"Call the agency," he directed. "If you can't locate anyone, let me know, and I'll try myself."

"Yes, Doctor," the head nurse said meekly. And then she added: "Oh, Mr.

Boone seems to be very uneasy this morning. He has been inquiring for you."

A pained look crossed Dr. Rodman's fat face. "Again!" he exclaimed. "Doesn't he know I've just brought in a seriously hurt patient!"

Emma Graham made no reply to this as she searched through her list of phone numbers. It wasn't more than five minutes later that the little doctor came back to the desk, looking wan and completely let down.

"I must discuss this with Dr. Brayley," he muttered. "I simply cannot cope with this man!" And he went over to take the elevator downstairs.

Edna was busy looking after the needs of some of the other patients and didn't find out what had happened until nearly a half-hour later. Then Emma Graham brought her up to date.

"One of the maids brought him in some coffee." The head nurse chuckled. "Boone made her so nervous she wound up spilling it over him and his bed. He's furious. Rodman has given up. He's got Dr. Halliday in there with him now."

As they talked, the light from Horace Boone's room flashed on. Emma Graham glanced at it and told Edna: "Better go and see what's happening."

When she went into the millionaire's room, Dr. Rodman was on one side of the fat man's bed and Preston Halliday on the other. For the first time since he'd entered the hospital, Horace Boone had a smile on his balloon face.

He was saying: "Mighty interesting to meet you, Halliday. I heard about you from Komrad and Marven. Your lab did some independent testing of their new diabetic formula. They were most enthusiastic."

Preston Halliday humored the problem patient with a smile. "Nice to know that your work has been appreciated." He turned to Edna. "Nurse, I'm going to have Mr. Boone put on a new medication. It's written down here. Tell Mrs. Graham we'll start it at once." He handed her a slip.

Dr. Rodman nodded affirmation from across the bed. "Dr. Halliday and I both agree the patient requires it."

It was the first time Edna had ever known the egotistical Rodman to agree with any other doctor.

Emma Graham studied the slip, and her lip curled derisively. "Tranquillizers," she said. "Too bad Rodman couldn't have thought about using them long ago. Maybe now we'll have a little quiet and order on the floor."

Edna said: "Mr. Boone seems very impressed by Dr. Halliday."

"I suppose because Halliday has been a lab worker," the head nurse guessed. "He thinks they are on the same team."

When Edna finished her day at the hospital, it was still raining. Mel, who was leaving at the same time, had promised to drive her home.

The rain was not quite so heavy, and by the time Mel let her off only a few drops were falling. When she went into the house, she found it empty. But Bernice left a note for her on the hall table in her familiar scrawl: "Jim phoned and wants you to call him at the house."

She picked up the phone and slowly dialed Jim's number. It rang for a few times, and then Jim's familiar voice answered.

"Bernice left your message," she said.

"I wanted to talk to you early," Jim told her. "The weather should be good tomorrow, and I thought we might make up a party and go out in the boat. Eric and Nancy can make it. And doesn't Bernice see a lot of Elliot Roger at the playhouse? She could come and bring him."

Edna hesitated. She disliked being on

parties with her stepmother. It nearly always produced difficult moments. But Bernice didn't get many chances to enjoy a big cabin cruiser such as the Boones'.

Finally she said: "I'll speak to her about it. I can let you know later."

"Fine," he said. "I'll be picking you up for the club dance."

"You want to go tonight?" she asked.

"Sure. We always go," he said. And then, suddenly aware of her lack of enthusiasm, he asked: "What's wrong. You sound different."

"Do I?" She felt her cheeks flush guiltily. "It's nothing. I'm just a bit tired. I'll see you tonight."

Chapter Seven

Edna had changed into a flowered print housecoat and was setting the dining room table for their evening meal when her stepmother arrived. The blonde woman burst into the paneled room with a pleased smile on her face.

"Did you know we're both invited for a sail on the Boones' yacht tomorrow?" Bernice asked.

She put down the last plate and smiled at her stepmother. "I heard a rumor of it on the phone from Jim a little while ago."

Bernice nodded happily. "I'm so thrilled!" she exclaimed. She was wearing her favorite white dress again, with purple necklace and earrings in a startling, if not too tasty, contrast.

Edna stood in the kitchen doorway. "If the weather clears, it could be fun. Is your friend from the playhouse coming as well?"

"Elliot Roger?" Bernice said. "Yes. He is. And Eric is bringing along Nancy Carrington." She hesitated and gave Edna a knowing smile. "I think there's something awfully serious between those two."

Edna laughed. "Well, at least they're giving the town a juicy topic of scandal."

"I really mean it. I think Eric is in love with that girl."

"But does she care anything about him?"

Bernice showed amazement. "Any girl who wouldn't care about the Boone millions must be crazy!"

"Not everyone thinks the same way," Edna pointed out. "She may be serious about her acting career. And Eric is much too possessive to consider sharing her with a job."

Her stepmother shook her head glumly. "All I can say is you girls don't know a good thing when you have it. You treat Jim as coolly as if you had a dozen suitors on a string, which you don't! And she acts as if she were Audrey Hepburn, which she isn't! You two should get wise."

Edna had heard enough. She went on out to the kitchen as her stepmother continued her oration about the madness of not jumping at the chance to marry a millionaire.

After dinner, in great good humor, the blonde woman pushed Edna toward the stairs. "You go up and get ready for your date," she insisted. "I can clean up without any help."

Edna smiled and started up the stairs. "I don't have the strength to argue about it," she said. "We had those people from the car accident today, and even the regular patients kept us hopping."

Upstairs she took a longer time than usual with her hair and found a suitable small comb with a pattern of rhinestones to set it off. She selected an attractively styled turquoise dress. It had an oriental flair, with a small collar and slits on the sides of the slim skirt. Jim called it her "Chinese" dress and had mentioned liking it.

Bernice let the big blond man in when he arrived. When Edna came downstairs, he was seated in the living room having a cigarette. He rose as she came in, a pleasant smile on his face. Bernice, who was standing near the doorway, glanced at Edna's dress with appraising eyes.

"I think she looks lovely in that." She turned to Jim. "Don't you agree?"

"I like it very much," Jim said. And then, gallantly: "But she looks great in just about anything."

Edna laughed. "Just about anything is what I'll have to wear on the boat tomorrow if we go. I haven't a suitable thing that's clean."

Bernice said: "She doesn't have to worry, does she, Jim? It's an outing; not a fashion show."

"Sure," Jim agreed heartily. "Don't give it a thought."

Bernice spoke to Edna. "I liked that other dress you wore, the one you had on the night you went out with Dr. Halliday."

There was an innocent smile on Bernice's face as she said this, but Edna knew she'd done it deliberately.

In the moment of silence that followed, Edna glanced at Jim and saw that his face had lost its smile. While he didn't look actually angry, he did look uncomfortable. She knew that he'd heard and that he wasn't pleased. She decided to ignore the remark altogether.

She smiled at Jim. "I think we'd better be getting on."

When they had gotten into his car and were alone, he said: "Well, I guess Bernice really let the cat out of the bag."

Edna glanced at him with teasing eyes. "Are you really bothered because I went out for an evening with Preston Halliday?"

"Don't you think I should be?" he asked, turning on the motor.

"Frankly, no," she said. "But then you sometimes take it into your head to be foolishly jealous when you have no reason."

He gave her a rueful smile. "I'll try hard to behave."

And he did. He immediately began to talk about his boat as they drove on in the direction of the country club. He'd had some work done on the motor and was anxious to try it out the next day. Edna had never been in it and found herself interested as he described its very good points.

Not until they had arrived at the country club and several dances did he mention Preston Halliday again. They were seated on a divan, one of many that were placed along the walls of the large room where the dancing took place. The orchestra was taking a break, and it was a natural time for conversation.

"By the way," Jim's face was wrinkled in a speculative frown, "this Dr. Halliday must be quite a man. Dad's very much impressed by him. I went to the hospital for a short visit on my way to your place tonight. Dad mentioned having had a talk with Halliday and said Halliday had helped him a lot."

"He did see your father this morning," Edna said. "I think your father knew him from some research job he'd done."

"Conducted a survey for a rival house," Jim said, "and did a mighty good job, from what I hear." He paused. "You know, from the way Dad talked to me about him, I wouldn't be surprised if he asks him to go to work for us."

Edna gave him a surprised glance. "Dr. Halliday work for you?"

Jim laughed. "Why not? He's a research man. Nearly every big drug company has some specialist from the medical profession on their staff. We've been looking for the right man for some time. I think Dad sees him in Halliday."

Edna looked dubious. "I think your father would be wasting his time to ask him. Preston Halliday is a very dedicated man. I don't think he'd leave his place in the active field for a commercial position, however good the offer might be."

"If Dad makes an offer, it will be a good one," Jim told her.

"But wouldn't you be better off with some first-rate chemist?" she asked.

"No." Jim was emphatic. "Today you need a medical degree for window dressing. And there's lots of real work to do as well. We've followed the leader in our field for a long time. We should be developing some products ourselves, and a talented research man like Halliday could be the key."

Edna smiled. "You're certainly entitled to try to get him. But I know what his answer will be."

"He might surprise you," Jim said. "Dad is pretty persuasive, and we do have plenty to offer as far as salary is concerned. I doubt if any private hospital or lab could match us."

"I don't think money would enter into it," Edna said. "He wouldn't think of wasting his talent that way."

"Well, wait and see," Jim said.

The orchestra came back and resumed playing, and they joined the other dancers gradually filling the floor.

Later in the evening, when the dance had ended and Jim had driven her home, they sat for a time in the car in front of her place. Jim turned toward her in the darkness. "You know I'm very much in love with you, Edna," he said quietly.

"I know, Jim." She gave a soft sigh.

His arm slipped around her, and he pulled her close to him. "You haven't given me an answer yet. When will you say you'll marry me?"

She looked up into his face. "I don't

know." She spoke barely above a whisper.

He studied her with puzzled eyes. "What's wrong with Eric and me? He's getting no place with Nancy Carrington, and you keep putting me off!"

"No, Jim," she rebuked him. "I'm very fond of you."

"You take a strange way of showing it. I suppose you're fond of this Halliday as well?"

"I like him, yes," Edna admitted. "But I doubt if I'd accept his proposal any quicker than I have yours. I'm not ready to make my mind up yet."

"When do you think you will be?" he asked in a patient yet slightly taut voice.

She smiled. "I'll know. It's not something you can predict or force. Just give me some time."

"I'll do that," he said, "providing you don't waste it on Halliday." And with this he leaned close and gave her a long, fervent kiss.

She finally pulled back from him with a small gasp. "I think you are pretty persuasive yourself," she said. "You're not being fair."

He stared at her fondly. "I'm not worried about the rules any more. I just want to win."

"Winning is important only under the right conditions," she reminded him. "And the right condition in this case is love."

"I'm sure enough for my part," he said.

"Then give me the chance to be equally sure."

"All right, Edna," he said. "We'll play it your way, even though I know I shouldn't."

On this bleak note of compromise they said good night. They discussed plans for the next day, and it was decided that Jim would let Elliot Roger pick up both her and Bernice in his convertible. Then they'd drive to the dock and meet the others.

In the morning, Elliot Roger came by for them just before eleven. He was a distinguished, slim man, a few years older than Bernice, with an effete cast to his handsome features. He was wearing a beret, and he greeted them with drawling good humor.

"Ready to bound on the ocean blue, ladies," he said as they got in.

Bernice made a wry face. "I hope that it isn't too rough. I have a very poor stomach for the water."

Elliot Roger laughed. "Should be as calm as a millpond today. There isn't any kind of breeze."

"It is lovely and warm," Edna agreed.

"You'll find it cooler on the water," Bernice promised. "I've brought along a sweater."

She was wearing a bikini bathing suit that showed her figure off in a daring way. Over it she had on a beach dress in the same material with a tie to hold it in place. Edna knew the outfit must have cost a small fortune, and she'd never seen it before. In spite of Bernice's constant complaints about how poorly off she'd been left, she managed to have plenty to spend on clothes.

Edna wore a plain pair of blue shorts and a striped sweater top that was designed like an overblouse. She also had brought a white bathing suit with her in case she decided to use it.

On the way to the dock, Bernice and Elliot kept up a bantering conversation that seemed rather silly to her. But she busied herself watching the houses as they drove by, now and then smiling polite encouragement to one or the other as they continued their mock arguments. On reaching the docks, Elliot drove his car out as far as he could and then parked close to a loading shed. They walked the rest of the way until they came to a trim white cabin cruiser with contrasting mahogany trim.

Bernice glanced at Edna. "What a lovely craft!" she exclaimed.

Elliot Roger was visibly impressed. He shook his head in wonder. "I wouldn't mind having what that cost in my bank account!"

Jim, Nancy and Eric were already on board. Jim greeted them from its gleaming deck in white trousers, blue sports shirt and a white yacht cap. Edna found herself thinking that the big man looked very handsome. He helped them on board with genial courtesy and then went forward to check the motor before they cast off. Eric was dressed in a yachting outfit identical with his brother's, and Nancy also wore a pair of white slacks and a light blue pull-over sweater. She looked casual and carefree. Her expression behind sunglasses seemed gay enough, and Edna decided they should have a reasonably good day with everybody in high spirits.

She hadn't counted on Bernice and her stomach. They hadn't gotten out a mile before the blonde woman complained of feeling ill. The strange part of it was that it was true. Even though there was only the mildest of swells, Bernice had a green look. She moved far to the back of the boat and stood by the rail, while a distressed Elliot

Roger stood with an arm around her waist attempting to be of some help.

Edna stayed with Jim near the wheel. The big man grinned at her. "I'll bet you're worried about Bernice."

She glanced back at her stepmother, still bent over the rail, then turned to Jim again with a mischievous glint in her eyes. "At least this way she'll stay decently quiet."

"First thing you know she'll be saying we plotted against her," he joked. "I don't think Elliot Roger is having much fun."

"It won't put him in the most romantic mood," Edna agreed, looking back again and catching a glimpse of the troubled features of the leading man as he attempted to comfort Bernice.

For most of the cruise Eric and Nancy stayed up front by themselves. They seemed in a very loving mood and acted as if they resented any intrusion on their privacy. Edna was satisfied that they were on good terms again. She hoped somehow they'd manage to remain that way. But with two people so temperamental and so much in love, this was doubtful.

Jim was occupied most of the time with the operation of the sleek cruiser. When Edna prepared an outdoor meal of hot dogs and French fries in the small but well-equipped galley, everyone but Bernice ate heartily. She staggered back to her established position at the rail and looked greener than ever. It was chiefly on her account that they came back early and Jim tied up at the wharf.

Bernice had Elliot Roger drive her home at once. Edna and Jim stayed on the boat after Eric and Nancy left to go somewhere on their own. Jim had some work to do with the steering gear, and Edna sat and watched with interest as he skillfully went about tearing it down and making the required repairs. When he finished, it was time to go somewhere to eat. They chose a modest dockside restaurant that had good sea food, and then Jim drove her home. Bernice was in bed when she got home, and Edna was glad. She hurried by without knocking and got ready to retire early herself.

The next morning was busier than the usual Monday at the hospital. There was a special air of tension on floor three, because this was the morning of David Danton's operation. Mel Parker and one of the nurses from downstairs helped get him ready. Edna was busy with other patients. The three accident victims were in much better condition, and one of them expected to be discharged before the day was out.

Mrs. Danton arrived a quarter of an hour before her husband was scheduled to be taken downstairs for his eight o'clock operation. She flashed Edna a weak smile. "I had to force myself to come," she said. "I'm such a coward. I don't know how I can talk to him without breaking down."

Edna took her arm as they went along the corridor to the columnist's room. "You're taking the wrong attitude," she said briskly. "This operation is to help your husband, not hurt him."

"He might die on the table." Mrs. Danton began to sniffle.

"Nonsense," Edna said. "I'll guarantee that won't happen. With modern methods, there's very little strain on a patient. And you have a fine, careful surgeon, even if this is a small hospital in a small town."

Too late Edna realized she had made a mistake by saying this. Mrs. Danton gave her a frightened look.

"I told him!" the columnist's wife wailed. "I warned him not to go ahead with it here. But he insisted. Now it's too late!" She thrust her hankie against her mouth in a dramatic gesture.

Edna stopped with her a few feet from the door of her husband's room. She looked to make sure the door was closed.

"I can't let you go in and upset him," she told the astonished woman: "You have a fine husband, and he deserves your courageous support. Don't go in there unless you can control yourself."

Mrs. Danton gave her an indignant glare. "I'm his wife!" she gasped.

"No one denies that," Edna said grimly. "Can you behave properly?"

The woman nodded, too taken back to concentrate on her grief.

David Danton was in bed when they entered and greeted them with a weary smile. "I've been prepared like the fatted calf," he said.

Mrs. Danton bent over and kissed him. Then she glared at Edna. "I'd have gotten here sooner," she said in a tone of self-pity, "but I was delayed in the corridor."

"Plenty of time," he said. He smiled at Edna. "You'll get a rest from me today. They tell me I'll be enjoying myself in the recovery room."

"They won't keep you there long," she promised.

"Well, at least it has an optimistic name," he said.

Their conversation was interrupted by the appearance of Edna's uncle, Dr. Charles Brayley. The middle-aged surgeon smiled gravely as he entered. "This is quite a farewell party they're giving you, Danton," he said.

The columnist laughed lightly. "Not a large crowd, but select."

The attendants entered, and a moment later, with a last faint smile and a wave of his hand, David Danton was wheeled out of the room. As soon as he'd been taken away, his wife sat down in the easy chair and began to weep.

Edna came across the room to the woman and touched her shoulder. "If that helps, it's all right now. I didn't want you to do it while he was still here."

The woman in the chair paid no attention to her, and Edna decided that it would be best to leave her alone for the time being.

She hesitated at the room door. "I'll be back soon, Mrs. Danton," she said, and went out.

At the desk, Head Nurse Emma Graham greeted her with a solemn look. "I suppose they'll be starting in a few minutes," she said.

"Yes, I suppose so," Edna agreed quietly. She glanced up at the big clock overhead with its large black figures. It was three minutes to eight.

Chapter Eight

"They could be busy down there a long time," was Head Nurse Emma Graham's comment.

"I know," Edna said.

The nurse with the glasses gave her a searching look. "How's his wife?"

She shrugged. "You know her type. I had to give her quite a talking to before she went inside to see him. I know she resented it. When I left her she was crying."

Emma Graham nodded. "What you have to do you have to do. I'll send Mel in to her with a happy-tablet cocktail of some sort. She needs something."

"She'd probably react better to Mel now," Edna agreed. And then, as an after thought: "Before you give her anything you'd better find out what she took before she came here."

The head nurse stood up. "Wise girl," she said. "She may have already loaded up on tranquillizers or who knows what! We don't want her collapsing on our hands to add to the problem."

As they were talking, the light for

Horace Boone's room went on.

Edna glanced at it. "Want me to take it?"

Emma Graham nodded. "That will leave Mel free, and I can send her in to see what is happening with the Danton woman."

Edna hurried down the corridor to Horace Boone's room, not certain with what problem he would present her. But she found him in a good state of mind. He smiled at her like a beneficent Buddha and said: "Would you please close the window, Nurse? I felt I needed some air. But now the breeze is too cool for me."

She went over and quickly adjusted the window, then turned to him with an amused look. "Is there anything else?"

He nodded. "Yes. I'm expecting the New York papers. Have they come yet?"

"No," she told him. "They usually are delivered about nine."

He looked unhappy. "That's pretty late, isn't it?"

"We're a long way from New York," she pointed out. "They fly down the early morning editions. Sometimes when the weather is bad, they can be a day late getting here."

The fat man glanced toward the window. "Well, it's fine enough today."

She smiled. "I'll see you get them as

soon as they arrive." And she started for the door.

"Say," he called after her, "you're new here, aren't you?"

"Not really," she said. "I've even been in to see you several times before."

Horace Boone registered interest. "You're not Charles Brayley's niece?"

"That's right," she agreed.

"Then you know my son, Jim!"

"Very well," Edna said. "I was going to mention it to you when you came in, but you seemed rather ill."

The fat man's chins quivered as he chuckled. "You mean rather bad-tempered. My nerves were in a state. I feel better now, thanks to young Halliday."

"I'm glad," she said, anxious to get away but not wanting to seem abrupt.

"Wasting his time around here," Horace Boone announced. "He has the talent to go places." And then, coming back to the subject: "Jim has told me a lot about you. You're pretty good friends."

"We've known each other a long time," Edna said.

The old man smiled knowingly. "Tell him I approve of his taste." He chuckled, and the chins shook again. "Don't forget those papers when they come."

"I'll bring them in myself," she promised with a smile, and left the room.

She made routine calls on the two accident patients who were sharing room 306, then went to the desk.

Mel and Emma Graham were conferring. The head nurse gave her an inquiring glance. "How are Rodman's two old harpies?"

Edna shook her head hopelessly. "One of them is feeling so much better she's causing a row. I think she's ready to leave."

"No doubt about that," Emma Graham agreed. "I'll tell Dr. Rodman when he comes in."

Mel Parker's angular face lit up with a teasing smile. "What made you abuse poor Mrs. Danton?"

Edna looked startled. "Did she say I abused her?"

Mel nodded. "She says you're the most coldhearted person she's ever met. I gave her one of Mother Graham's potions, and she's relaxing now."

Edna glanced up at the clock and saw that it was just past eight-thirty. By now the surgeons would be making their findings on David Danton.

She said: "Have the papers come yet? Mr. Boone has been asking for them."

"Not yet," Emma Graham said. "We've lots to worry about besides the morning papers." She glanced at her desk. "There's a gerebro-vascular accident coming in. A patient from Brighton. One of Dr. Penny's cases."

Edna recalled the thin, elderly doctor from the neighboring town. He was a hard-working, competent man but completely colorless. He had few close friends at the hospital and was not a frequent visitor there. Only when a case was too serious for him to cope with did they hear from him.

The morning papers finally came, and they were early. It was only a quarter to nine when Edna took the promised copies down to Horace Boone's room.

The millionaire was delighted to get them. He said: "You've made my morning a success."

"We like to see our patients happy," Edna told him. "It's one of the main ingredients in a successful recovery."

He gave her a shrewd look. "You don't seem particularly happy yourself this morning," he said. "That smile of yours is a little pinched."

She stared at him in surprise. "Is that really true?"

"It is," he declared. "And you seem in a

pretty tense mood as well."

"I didn't realize it showed so plainly," she said. "I am rather upset. A favorite patient of mine is in the O.R. now. I suppose I'll feel this way until I hear the report on the operation."

Horace Boone was impressed. "Well," he said, "I had no idea you nurses took so much interest."

She gave him a wry smile. "We are human," she said. "And sometimes we discover we have involved ourselves much too deeply in a case. I'm afraid that's what's happened to me now."

"Who is the patient?" Horace Boone asked.

"David Danton, the columnist," Edna said. "You must have heard of him."

The millionaire looked shocked. "I read his stuff every day in this paper." He lifted up one of New York papers for her to see. He thumbed through it and opened the pages to one with a two-column heading over a recognizable photo of a smiling Danton. He said: "There's a column of his in here today as usual. And he's downstairs in the operating room!"

"He keeps a few weeks ahead," Edna explained.

The old man stared at the paper. "Beats all." Then to Edna: "Well, I wish him luck.

He's a good reporter."

Back in the corridor, Edna found herself feeling somewhat ashamed that she'd let her worry about Danton's operation show so plainly. It wasn't fair to her other patients.

Just as she reached the end of the corridor, she saw her uncle coming out of the elevator. At the sight of him, she felt her heart miss a beat. She looked from him to the big overhead clock and saw that it was only four minutes past nine. The operation had lasted a mere hour! That could mean only one thing, and she didn't want to think about it.

Charles Brayley came toward her with a grave face. "Is Mrs. Danton still in the room?" he asked.

"Yes," Edna said.

"How is she?"

"Mrs. Graham sent her in some tranquillizers some time ago," Edna told him. "I think she must be all right."

"Good." Her uncle sighed deeply. His face was weary, and she was aware how deeply etched were the lines about his mouth and the frown wrinkles on his forehead.

She ventured: "How did it go?"

His eyes met hers grimly. "I opened him

134

and I closed him."

"No!" she exclaimed in a low voice.

"There was nothing else to do," her uncle said. "It's hopeless. No surgeon can help him now. It's spread everywhere."

"Then it was cancer?"

He shrugged. "I'd definitely say so even without the lab report. Perhaps a series of radiation treatments might shrink it some, although I doubt it."

"And if radiation doesn't help now, how long will he have?"

Her uncle considered. "A random guess would be three or four months. I mean three or four months of steadily deteriorating condition."

"So that's it," she said softly. "Now you've got to tell her."

"Yes." He nodded. "Now I've got to tell her. Sometimes I think this is the worst part of it. I was tempted to send Halliday up, but that would hardly be fair. I'm afraid he found today's experience unpleasant enough as it was."

"A little different from the remoteness of the research lab," she said.

"Exactly," her uncle said. "I should have had someone else in there with me today. There was nothing at all he could do. A frustrating experience."

"Perhaps he will gain from it in the long run," Edna suggested.

"I doubt that." Her uncle glanced toward the room where Danton's wife was waiting and sighed again. He said: "I think you'd better come in with me."

She held back. "I don't know. I had to be very firm with her earlier this morning, and she resented it. Perhaps you'd better take one of the other nurses."

He shook his head. "I'd rather have you. And it might be necessary for you to be firm with her again in her own best interests."

With misgivings Edna followed her uncle down the corridor and into the room. Mrs. Danton rose expectantly as the doctor entered, a wavering smile on her face. "It didn't take you so long after all, Doctor," she said, apparently not aware of Edna in her excitement.

Dr. Brayley went up to her. "No, it didn't take us as much time as we'd expected. But I'm afraid that's not always a hopeful sign."

The woman stared at him. "No?"

He spoke slowly so she would be sure to understand. "Your husband is a very ill man, Mrs. Danton. We did only minor surgery. I'm afraid his condition is too complicated for us to help, although there is a chance that radiation treatments combined with chemical therapy might do some real good."

Mrs. Danton's eyes opened wide at the implication of his words, and she sat down again. She spoke in a low voice. "It was cancer."

"That is probably true," Dr. Brayley said.

She looked up at him. "How long will he have?"

"No one can say definitely," Dr. Brayley told her. "If radiation helps, it could brighten the entire outlook. If it doesn't, I don't think he can live longer than a few months."

Now Mrs. Danton turned her attention to Edna. "What's she doing here?" she asked.

Edna's uncle showed slight embarrassment. "I thought you might need her."

Mrs. Danton's tone and expression were filled with sarcasm. "I certainly hope not."

Dr. Brayley became briskly professional. "Your husband will be in the recovery room until morning. I suggest you go home and rest."

She raised her eyes to meet his again. "How long will you keep him here?"

"He should be able to leave in a fort-night," Dr. Brayley said. "Meanwhile, I can make arrangements for radiation treatments so there will be no delay in getting them under way. I would suggest M.I.T. in Boston. They have a strong unit there."

Mrs. Danton nodded as if all this were not important. Then she said: "How am I going to tell him?"

Dr. Brayley's voice became sharp. "Tell him?"

"Yes." The shallow-minded woman gave him a doleful look. "How can I tell him that he has cancer and has only a few months to live?"

He looked at her sternly. "Mrs. Danton, it is my belief that your husband should not be told."

She stared at him in surprise. "Not be told! I can't carry it alone. It's too much."

"I think it is your duty to carry this burden, Mrs. Danton," Dr. Brayley said gravely. "I dislike having to ask you to do so. But it is in your husband's best interests."

"Best interests!" The woman laughed bitterly. "He's going to die of this thing anyway. How can you talk about best interests?"

"No one," Dr. Brayley said quietly but

firmly, "can predict what is going to happen to your husband. He is gravely ill, and I am unable to help. But we can hope for help from other sources, as I've explained. One of the most important factors is your husband's state of mind. He was nervous and apprehensive when he came to us, and I think we have helped him conquer his fears to a degree. If you face him now with the news that he is a terminal cancer patient, I'm certain it will harm his chances of responding to treatment."

"It's not fair," she wailed. "I can't keep up a pretense. It's too much to ask of me."

"Not even to help save your husband's life, or at least give him a little time longer in reasonable comfort?" the old doctor asked.

"He'll know," Mrs. Danton insisted. "If you suggest radiation treatments, how can he help knowing?"

"I will tell him I think the operation cleared up his trouble," Dr. Brayley said, "but I want him to have the radiation therapy to make sure that nothing was left."

"I call it a cruel lie," Mrs. Danton whimpered.

"It is what I advise," Dr. Brayley said. "We have no right to rob anyone of his

139

hope for life. Neither you nor I can know what God's plan is for your husband. I suggest you think that over. In my long experience I have found that dying people know their condition without it being underlined for them. The unspoken truth will almost certainly be an accepted thing between you before the end. But I still say it should remain unspoken."

Mrs. Danton seemed to gain some control of herself. She dabbed at her eyes with her hankie and then stood up. "I'll think over what you have told me, Doctor. I don't agree with you, but I will try to bring myself to do what you feel is best."

Dr. Brayley said: "The nurse will see you safely downstairs."

Mrs. Danton turned away haughtily. "No, thank you!"

"Then I will do it myself," he said, taking her arm. On his way to the door, he threw Edna an understanding glance.

When she went back to the desk, she told Emma Graham what had taken place in the room. The head nurse listened with sympathy. She, too, had come to like the columnist.

She said: "I'm not surprised. I had a feeling it would be like this from the first."

"Uncle felt terribly about it," Edna said,

"and I guess Dr. Halliday did, too."

"They always do." Nurse Graham looked down at her desk with its litter of papers. "Well, all that can be done now is to get him on his feet so the radiation treatments can be given without too much delay."

Mel Parker came up to them and said in a low voice: "Here comes California's most eminent and gifted medico!"

Dr. Rodman was just emerging from the elevator. He was immaculately neat in a dark, pin-striped suit with the usual white flower in his buttonhole.

He came up to them briskly with a broad smile on his fat face. "Good morning, ladies," he said with a slight bow. "How are all my patients this morning?"

"One of your accident cases in the double room is doing so well she's causing a disturbance," Head Nurse Graham said grimly. "I think she should be discharged."

"Ah, yes." Dr. Rodman teetered gently back and forth. "I will see her."

"We'd like to move the other patient into 322," Emma Graham continued. "It's a three-bed room, but your patient isn't very ill. We have a stroke case coming in from Brighton, and I'm trying to clear a private room."

Dr. Rodman hesitated and cleared his

throat. "This is rather awkward. I don't think my patient will agree to be moved. She only accepted the double room because she is sharing it with her friend."

"I'm afraid you'd better take it up with Dr. Brayley," Emma Graham said firmly. "It was his suggestion that I move her."

"I will see Dr. Brayley," Dr. Rodman said. "Is he still in the O.R.?"

Edna shook her head. "No. He was up here a few minutes ago talking with Mrs. Danton. I imagine he'll be in his office now."

The squat doctor regarded them all with speculative eyes. "Indeed?" he said. "He must have had a very short time in the O.R." He waited for them to fill in the facts he obviously wanted, but none of them said anything.

He turned to go, his face suddenly mottled with a deep crimson hue, and finally asked: "What about the patient in 310?"

"Doing very well, I believe," Emma Graham said coolly. "You remember, she has the private nurse you arranged for her."

Dr. Rodman nodded and marched down the corridor in the direction of room 310.

Chapter Nine

For the rest of the day Edna went about her work in a subdued mood. It proved to be another difficult day, and only once did she catch a fleeting glimpse of Dr. Preston Halliday when they were both in the cafeteria for lunch. He was on his way out as she seated herself at a table with Mel Parker, and he stopped for just a moment to smile at her wanly and say: "I was thinking of phoning you tonight."

She looked up at his handsome, sensitive face. "I'll be home all evening," she said.

"Good!" He smiled again and was on his way.

Mel Parker's angular face wore an expression of frank envy. The blonde girl said plaintively: "How do you do it? He's only been here a few days, and already you have him twisted around your little finger!"

"That," Edna laughed, "is the worst kind of exaggeration. I'm only trying to help him get adjusted to Farmingham."

"If you'll pardon a friend asking," Mel said tartly, "how does good old Jim Boone feel about you adjusting Dr. Halliday?"

Edna looked down at her plate. "Actually, he's been very understanding. I'm very fond of Jim, and he knows it."

Mel started to eat her dinner with a sigh. "Well, I wish you'd soon decide which one you're fonder of and give the rest of us poor girls a chance."

Edna studied the blonde girl with amused eyes. "You're always discussing my romantic affairs. Let me hear something about yours. Didn't you used to see a lot of some fellow named Elmer?"

Mel paused with a piece of roast beef speared on her fork. "Elmer Puddington! I haven't thought of him in the longest while! He was a salesman; worked out of Boston. Sold bolts and nuts. Turned out to be one. Married some raven-haired beauty from Portland."

"I'm sorry," Edna said, genuinely disappointed.

The blonde girl shrugged. "Don't be! I'm not. It was probably my lucky day when he met that Portland gal. All he ever talked about was hardware. You know that can get very tiresome. He sent me a magazine subscription for Christmas one year. *The Hardware Journal*! I began to worry after that!"

144

"Well, there are lots more around," Edna said.

Mel opened her eyes wide. "I wish you'd find one for me. There are not schools of them swimming by me."

Edna smiled. "You just imagine that."

"No" Mel shook her head. "Just as soon as they find out I have a kid brother and a widowed mother, they wheel around in the opposite direction!"

"I have a stepmother who is a widow," Edna reminded the blonde girl.

Mel laughed. "You must be kidding! Your widowed mother and mine are just about a hundred light years apart. My mother is close to sixty and a semi-invalid, and yours is about thirty and a blonde bombshell. You have all the luck!"

"Sometimes I don't think so," Edna said ruefully.

After lunch Dr. Penny brought in his stroke patient. He was an elderly man, and he was still in an unconscious state. In his usual modest way the Brighton doctor looked after the details without causing any sort of excitement. Edna saw by the stroke victim's chart that he was on the critical list.

Emma Graham told the gentlemanly country doctor: "I had a hard time clearing

306 for you, Doctor, but I finally managed."

He smiled modestly. "I'm really grateful. You're always so good to me here."

"No trouble at all," the head nurse blithely assured him. "Dr. Rodman's patient isn't seriously ill, and it was only right she should move out."

Edna's shift ended, and on her way out of the hospital she stopped by her uncle's office. He was in the process of seeing Dr. Penny to the door when she came by. The two men were apparently having an earnest discussion of the stroke case.

Edna's uncle gave her a nod of greeting. Then, turning to Dr. Penny, he said: "You've met my niece, of course?"

"Yes." The Brighton doctor smiled. "And she's a credit to you, Charles."

"I'm afraid," Edna said, "that I'm in the position of the boss' daughter. I can do no wrong."

The country doctor shook his head. "Not at all. I'm judging you purely on your merits." He turned to her uncle. "I'll be on call if there should be any sharp change in the patient's condition. Otherwise I'll be here early in the morning."

"I'll keep you advised," Charles Brayley promised.

Dr. Penny nodded to her and went out. Her uncle turned with a sigh. "Well, it's been one of those days."

"How is David Danton?" she asked.

"The recovery room reports him in good shape," her uncle advised. "He'll recover from the operation quickly enough. There was so little done. It's afterward that worries me."

"Mrs. Danton seemed very anxious to tell him about his condition," she said.

"I know." Dr. Brayley frowned. "That woman is badly mixed up and quite selfish. I hope she saw the sense in what I told her today."

"I wouldn't call her dependable."

"I know it." He sighed. "All we can do is try and get Danton in a strong enough frame of mind so that nothing she can say or do will bother him too much."

"Do you think that's possible?"

Her uncle raised his eyebrows. "I've managed it in other cases. But Danton did come here in a bad state of fear. He's better now, of course, but it wouldn't take much to make him revert back."

Edna surprised herself by saying firmly: "He deserves a chance to live or at least enjoy what is left of his life."

Dr. Brayley patted her arm. "You really

are concerned," he said gently. "Don't worry about it. I'm giving Danton special attention. Go home and forget this for a time."

Edna arrived at the brown house with its shading elms determined to get her mind off hospital doings for a while at least. As it turned out, Bernice had this neatly arranged for her. The first surprise was the discovery of her stepmother in the kitchen, presiding over the stove.

"I have a nice stew on." She smiled brightly at Edna, looking not the least bit domestic in a chic blue suit. The one thing she enjoyed cooking was a stew. When she occasionally took it upon herself to help with a meal, this was invariably the dish on which she settled.

Edna stared at her with disbelief. "This is wonderful," she said. "Your stews are always so good."

"Don't you worry about a thing," Bernice said grandly. "I've made some jelly for dessert, and I'll whip the cream. Let's not worry about calories for one night. You go upstairs and rest until dinner is ready."

"It's exactly what I'd like to do," Edna murmured, overwhelmed by her stepmother's sudden burst of activity. The blonde woman had been quiet and listless since the unhappy boat experience of Sunday.

"I'm going over to the playhouse tonight with one of the girls from the hospital aide group," Bernice went on. "Elliot Roger has a wonderful part in this week's show. So we'll have dinner early."

"Call me any time you're ready," Edna said, and walked away, still a bit dazed.

In the middle of Bernice's dinner, the blonde woman produced her second surprise for Edna.

Bernice glanced up from her plate to ask: "Are you sure you're really enjoying this, dear? I'm afraid I've put a bit too much salt in it."

It did have a salty flavor, but it was edible, and Edna had no desire to discourage her stepmother from further efforts. She smiled at her from across the dining room table. "It's fine for me," she said.

Bernice went on in a casual tone: "Oh, the art dealer from Boston came by today."

"Good," Edna said. She knew that her stepmother had written him.

"He took long enough coming," Bernice said with a hint of annoyance. "I've been after him for weeks. My cash is getting dreadfully low, and I hoped he might be able to move a few of your father's paintings."

"How did you make out?" Edna raised her head to inquire innocently.

The blonde woman's pretty face wrinkled in distaste. "You know what art dealers are like. He made a lot of vague promises, and the whole thing led nowhere."

"I'm sorry," Edna said.

"There was one thing," Bernice went on slowly, tentatively.

Edna rose to the bait before she realized what was happening. "What was that?" she asked with a smile.

Bernice glanced around at the portrait of Edna's father. "He was interested in that. Blair did it, you know. And he's having a vogue now."

Edna still didn't understand. She looked up at her father's portrait, studying the strong, intellectual face with a feeling of inner warmth. Often when she felt in low spirits, she would come into the room to stand by this image of her father for a few minutes. It was surprising how much it helped.

She said softly: "It's a wonderful bit of work. I value it more than anything else we own."

It was Bernice's turn to show surprise. She said: "Really! I didn't think you prized it that much."

Edna nodded dreamily, still absorbed in her study of the portrait. "It's as though it were part of Dad, a very tangible part of him, still with us."

Bernice gave the portrait another quick glance. "I think the eyes are too close together," she said. And then, turning back to Edna uneasily: "I suppose you understood what I meant just now about the dealer. He wasn't merely interested in the portrait; he made me an offer of three thousand dollars for it."

At that moment Edna understood everything. She sat back from the table and stared at the blonde woman with consternation. She said: "You actually discussed a price with him?"

Bernice bit her lip. "Well," she said, "I didn't see any harm in that. I didn't know you had such a silly fixation about it."

"Silly fixation!" Edna echoed, so angry she found herself near tears. "That's the only portrait of Father I have, the only thing I have to remember him by except a few faded snapshots. And you actually considered selling it."

"Well," the blonde woman held her

ground as she reminded Edna stiffly, "your father left me half of the house and everything in it. I think I was within my rights."

"From your point of view you're always within your rights," Edna said, her voice rising. "Well, go ahead! Sell him your half of it. My half stays here!"

Bernice rolled her eyes. "Now you're talking like a crazy girl! I might have known you'd have one of your temper spells!"

"Me have a temper spell!" she cried, standing up and throwing her napkin on the table. "You're the one that's always complaining and having tantrums around here."

The blonde woman's anger was now aroused. "If your father had left me any kind of estate, I wouldn't be reduced to trying to peddle his paintings — paintings that no one wants, by the way!"

"You don't have to tell me about Dad's work," Edna retorted sharply. "I know its value. And that painting is not for sale under any conditions." She hurried out of the room and started upstairs.

Bernice followed her to the hallway. "I'll talk to my lawyer about this," she said. "You'll find out you have not the last word around here! You can't keep me penny-pinching this way when it isn't necessary!"

Edna didn't hear the rest. She'd rushed into her room and slammed and locked the door behind her. She threw herself down on the bed and realized she was quivering with rage. There were no tears in her eyes; she was too angry. And she felt humiliated that she'd fallen so easily into Bernice's little trap.

Later, she heard the horn of Bernice's friend as she came by in the car to pick Bernice up. There was the sound of the blonde woman's high heels clicking angrily downstairs and out the front door. The door closed with a loud bang, and the next thing Edna heard was Bernice's voice in a high-pitched, gay greeting to her friend as she got into the car.

Edna listened with disgust. After the car had driven off, she went downstairs, stood in the dining room and gazed up at the portrait. This time her eyes did brim with tears as she said softly: "It's no use clinging to this place any longer, Dad. Nothing is the same. I'm going away, and I'm taking you with me. She'll never sell you — never!"

Then she turned to the mess of dirty dishes on the table and in the kitchen where Bernice had left them. She slowly began to gather them up and take them out to wash.

She'd just put the last of the dishes away when the phone rang. Her heart gave a sudden surge as she decided it was probably Dr. Preston Halliday.

When she picked up the phone the young doctor's voice asked: "Any free time tonight?"

"As much as you like, sir," she said happily.

"I'm sick of driving," he said. "Is there any place we can walk around here? I mean some place pleasant to walk."

She considered, then said: "Yes, there is, about four blocks away. It's a small park, dedicated to Civil War heroes. It has a few benches and a pleasant cliff view of the river. I often have gone there by myself in the daytime."

"Sounds promising," he said. "I'll be around in fifteen minutes. Or is that too soon?"

"I'll be ready," she told him. "You don't have to dress very elaborately for a stroll in a park."

"That's one of the reasons I want to do something like that," he said. "I'm not in a mood for formality."

He came almost exactly fifteen minutes

after he called; she was already dressed and waiting on the front steps. She had put on a warm knit dress in a shade of light yellow and carried her light coat on her arm. He insisted on taking it from her and tossing it over his arm with his own topcoat.

"I hope you don't resent the idea of going for a walk," he said as they began to stroll leisurely in the direction of the small park.

She shook her head. "The air is wonderful tonight, and you get so little of it in a car."

"Spoken with true professional flair," he teased her. "Almost anyone could spot you as a prim young nurse."

Edna laughed. "Anyway, a nurse." She linked her arm in his. "Makes walking easier," she told him as they moved in step.

The summer evenings were beginning to get short, and it was cool as soon as the sun went down. It was just twilight as they walked slowly along the pleasant residential street with its well-painted houses set back under various kinds of shade trees. The houses in this district had been part of a development that had been built in Farmingham about thirty years before. Most of them were owned by well-to-do families, and the quiet, well-kept street reflected this.

Preston Halliday said: "You know all about this morning's fiasco in the operating room, of course."

She squeezed his arm with understanding. "It wasn't your fault or my uncle's. Poor Mr. Danton is just an unfortunate who discovered his illness too late."

"I hadn't assisted in several years." The young doctor's profile showed the grim expression on his face. "I went in there full of hope. I was almost physically ill when we had to sew him up again."

"I know how you must have felt," she said.

"I wonder." He glanced at her. "You know very little about me or my thinking, really. Anyhow, today convinced me of one thing. I want to get away from this sort of thing as soon as I can."

"I'm not surprised at that," she said. "You really belong in research."

He gave a short, bitter laugh. "I was no shining star there, either. Now I have the name of being a rebel, a poor prospect for team work. Not many labs will fight to secure my services. It's a small circle, and word gets around."

"Even when the report is unfair?" she

said, looking up at him. "You told me that you'd been stopped on two projects that might have amounted to something."

"The way I see it, I was," he said. "But the eminent gents who headed the labs will be listened to and my small protests be lost in the wind. So what does Dr. Preston Halliday do?"

She was almost afraid to let him go on. She remembered her conversation with Jim Boone. She knew from his father's attitude that he was ready to make Preston Halliday an offer. Had he already made it?

She tried to sound light and casual. But when she spoke the words came out in a strained, difficult tone. "What are your plans, Dr. Halliday?"

They'd now reached the small park. It was dark, and the street lamps had come on. Across the river they could see the lights of suburban Farmingham and the moving pinpoints of brightness that marked the passage of cars along the highway.

The monument, a Union officer with his hand on a sword, stood faintly illuminated by the rays of a modern blue floodlight. There were benches around the monument, set back under the shadows of giant elms. Preston Halliday led her to one of the benches, and they sat down.

He put the coats on the bench beside him and turned to her. "I had an interesting offer this morning."

"Yes?"

"Horace Boone wants me to take a position with his company," the young doctor said, looking directly at her. "It would pay more money than I've ever earned. And I would work about half as hard as I have since I graduated from college."

"Is that what you're looking for?" she asked. "An easy road through life?"

He shrugged. "Hardly! Both my parents and I made a lot of sacrifices so I could finish medical school. There were plenty of other ways I could have found to earn a fast buck, if that had been all I wanted. I came into medicine because I wanted, even needed, to help people. But up to now it seems to me I haven't done too well."

"I doubt if you'd find it such a wonderful idea," she said, staring at him with grave eyes. And then she smiled. "You don't even seem very happy talking about it now."

"So what else do I do?" he wanted to know. "Bat my stupid head around in some obscure lab and swallow my pride and my ideas when any stodgy superior glares at me? Or maybe you'd rather I stayed on at the hospital and sewed up patients who were too frightened to come to me in time to be saved."

"You can find a useful place in any of the medical worlds you choose," she told him softly. "You have the ability and the desire to be of service, and those are the most important two things in life. I think so, anyway."

He studied her with tender eyes. "You have a quality of honesty and a natural loveliness that I think are just as important; maybe more so."

He put his arm around her, and she came closer to him. In a moment their lips touched in an ecstatic kiss of solace rather than passion. A mutual feeling of oneness came to them as they sat there in the shadows. After a long while the kiss ended, and she regarded him tenderly.

"We discovered each other so quickly," she said.

"I've been in love with you since the first time we met at the hospital," he said. "I knew it was a crazy, impractical impulse, but I couldn't deny it."

She shook her head in hopeless wonder. "Where do we go from here?"

"I'll take Boone's offer, and we'll settle down to a healthy, wealthy life," he laughed.

She smiled at him. "No. I don't like the

sound of that. And then," she paused, "you've forgotten something quite important. I've had a Boone offer myself."

He stared at her with boyish concern. "From Jim Boone?"

"Yes." She looked away. "He asked me to marry him some time ago."

"And what was your answer?" Preston asked.

"I told him I needed time," she said, "that I hadn't made up my mind."

There was a short pause before he spoke again. Then he asked: "Have you made it up yet?"

She turned to face him. "I almost thought I had until a few minutes ago."

His face became grave. "You mean it might change things if I accepted Horace Boone's job?"

"I'm afraid so," she said. "I'm really afraid it would."

He gave her a cynical smile. "Then maybe we'd better both make sure of our futures. Let each of us accept a Boone offer!"

"Yes," she said slowly. "We could do that, I suppose." And she felt a wave of hopelessness surge through her as she realized the young doctor was more than half serious.

Chapter Ten

The following week passed quickly. Dr. Charles Brayley went away to a medical convention in Philadelphia and left Preston Halliday in complete charge of the hospital during his absence. Edna's uncle had indicated that he was counting on Dr. Rodman to assist the new man while he was attending the convention, but everyone knew this was a gesture to keep fussy Dr. Rodman in reasonable good humor while he was away.

Dr. Rodman took it seriously, however, and bounced about the hospital with new importance. The real work, of course, all fell on young Dr. Halliday's shoulders. Fortunately, he was able to cope with the situation, but he had to give the hospital almost all his waking moments. As a result, he and Edna had no opportunity to see each other. They did manage short conversations in the cafeteria when their mealtimes happened to coincide, but that was all.

One of the first things Edna did that week was to see a lawyer who had been one of her father's friends. Distinguished, graying Geoffrey Fisher had known her from childhood, so she had no hesitation about telling him her problems.

The veteran lawyer sat back thoughtfully behind the broad desk in the book-lined office and listened to her story. When she'd finished, he sat for a moment in silence.

Then, looking at her, he said, "It's not a very nice situation."

She smiled wryly. "That's an understatement."

His shrewd eyes studied her. "Why have you put up with it so long?"

"I don't know," she said. "I suppose because I hated to leave the house, and I felt I owed Bernice some loyalty because of Dad."

"Neither of those reasons seem valid now, do they?"

"No," she said firmly. "It would probably be the best thing for me to get away from the place. I've done all I can for Bernice. I just want some way out."

The lawyer stared up at the ceiling. "As I understand it, your father's will stipulated that the home was to be kept intact as long as either of you wanted to live there."

She nodded. "Yes. I suppose Dad wanted to be sure I'd always have a place if I needed it. And the same for Bernice."

"So if you want to leave and she refuses, there can be no question of selling the property and dividing the proceeds between you." He brought his eyes back to Edna.

"That seems to be the story," she said.

"In which case it would seem imperative that you somehow persuade your stepmother to see things your way. You must both agree to leave and instruct that the property be put up for sale."

"Yes," Edna said.

The lawyer sighed. "So it isn't actually a legal matter at this stage. I think you'll have to work this out some way between yourselves. After that, I'll be glad to act for you."

"Dad didn't think this arrangement would work out to hurt us," Edna said, "but it has. I know we'd both be better off on our own."

"The perfect will has yet to be written," the old lawyer said sadly. "Your father undoubtedly did his best, but he couldn't foresee what was going to happen. I judge there are still a number of his paintings to be sold."

"Quite a large number," Edna agreed. "I've left the disposal of them mainly to Bernice. But I think we could agree on a division of the paintings that are left."

He raised his eyebrows. "Then the question of values would enter into it. And that would be hard to pin down in the case of original art works. You would be best advised both to agree on a dealer. Let him handle the sales and divide the money equally afterward. That was your father's intention. But first, it seems, you must reach an agreement about all these matters with your father's widow."

Edna got up with a smile. "Thank you," she said. "At least now I know what has to be done."

On several evenings she tried to talk with Bernice, but the blonde woman always evaded the subject. Each time she found some excuse to retreat from the conversation. Edna knew why. The present arrangement suited her stepmother much better than it did her. She had made herself a slavey for the older woman and at the same time paid a lot of the bills.

One good result of their talks was that Bernice gave up nagging Edna to sell the portrait of her father. Edna decided she could be patient, but her mind was made up. Within the next few weeks she was going to force a showdown with the blonde woman. And when it was settled and she left to start on her own, the portrait of her father was going with her. She would gladly pay Bernice for her half of it.

At the hospital, things moved at a rapid pace. The second of the accident victims left, and the third woman was soon to go home with her leg still in a cast. Horace Boone was dismissed, and finally Dr. Rodman immediately became a much more lighthearted man. David Danton returned to his room and was soon rapidly mending from his operation.

When ever Mrs. Danton came on a visit, she made a point of ignoring and avoiding Edna. But she often stopped to chat with Emma Graham, smiling in her simpering way and revealing the mouthful of perfect teeth. The head nurse had come to detest the woman but somehow managed to conceal it.

David Danton was more friendly with Edna than ever and seemed to be in better spirits. She went into his room the following Monday morning to find him sitting up in bed with a book. He laid it down when she came in.

"Dr. Halliday tells me I can go back to my brother's place the end of the week," he told her happily.

"Wonderful," she said.

He sighed. "I'd like to stay there for a month or so until my strength returns," he said. "But they want me to go on to Boston for treatments."

"I'm sure my uncle has your best interests at heart," Edna told him.

"I suppose so," David Danton agreed. "He wants to be sure everything is cleared up. I think there's no need. I have a sort of inner feeling, call it intuition if you like, that I'm as all right as I'm ever going to be."

She hoped her compassion didn't show in her face. She tried to smile. "Just the same, I'd have the treatments."

"Oh, I intend to," the gaunt man assured her. "My wife seems very mixed up about it, but she's easily upset at best."

"I can understand," Edna said quietly.

The columnist looked at her seriously. "You've probably noticed that my wife is not — well, not what you'd call a sensitive person. She seems to have taken some vague dislike to you. I hope you'll forgive her and put it down to the trying crisis she's been through."

"Don't think anything about it," she said. "I haven't."

"I knew you wouldn't." He sighed. "But I wanted to speak frankly to you. I feel you

166

are my friend, one of the few real friends I've made since I've been here. And I think there should be frankness between friends, don't you?"

She made herself find words. "Friends should be considerate of each other."

He paused and gave her a strange look. "Yes, I suppose that's actually the same thing. As long as we're considerate of our friends, we shouldn't lose them."

Edna started toward the door. "If there's nothing else —" she said.

"There is something else," he said, "as long as we're being frank. One thing does worry me. I thought after the operation I'd be able to eat normally. In fact, your uncle practically promised I would. But I'm as bad as I was before."

"It takes time," she said carefully. "You must be patient until you're completely healed. The treatments should hasten your progress."

"I suppose that's it," he said. "I haven't completely healed yet." He smiled. "Impatience was always my major problem."

"A hospital is a good place to be cured of it," she told him.

"I've even been sitting here thinking about next summer," he went on, "making plans about what I'll do. First I'll march up to the hospital and say hello to everyone. Then I'll spend the rest of the summer on the beach. I haven't had a bit of sun or sea water. But next year will be different. And you'll have to promise to come down and visit us."

Edna wanted more than anything to get out of the room. "That's a promise," she told him quickly. "I have to run now; I'm way behind with my work." And with a desperately summoned smile, she left him.

That night she received an unexpected phone call from Jim Boone. The blond man suggested they go to the Wentworth for a dinner date and dancing. "The season is almost over," he said. "We might as well go while the place is still open."

She was glad of the prospect of an evening out. She wanted to forget the hospital completely. She said: "Fine. Come by about seven. Just blow your horn and I'll be right out."

He laughed. "You want to spare me from Bernice?"

"The situation is very touchy," she said. "I'll tell you about it when I see you."

Bernice was in the living room reading the evening paper when Edna came down, dressed to go out. The blonde woman looked at her curiously. "You didn't say anything about a date."

"Didn't I?" Edna said innocently. "I must have forgotten." She had decided to become as devious as her stepmother in pure self-defense.

The older woman was plainly dying to know where she was going and with whom but couldn't quite bring herself barefacedly to question her. She contented herself with observing: "Judging by your evening dress, you're going dancing."

"For a change," Edna said. She was standing by the front door waiting for Jim to drive up.

Her stepmother sighed. "Really, you haven't been very pleasant lately. I'm beginning to feel you're not happy here."

Edna glanced at her. "I thought I'd made that clear."

Bernice shook her head melodramatically. "You'll never be satisfied until you've broken this home up, after all the sacrifices I've made to keep it for you."

Edna felt like laughing in the blonde woman's face, but there would be little point in that.

Instead, she tried a new tactic. "I think we both have a lot to lose by staying here, especially you! You're not getting any younger, you know."

For once Bernice was speechless. She just sat staring at Edna with a shocked, angry expression. Edna never did find out what she might have been going to say in answer, because Jim's car came and she hurried out.

When she got into the car, she sank back against the seat and quivered with laughter. Jim gave her a curious side glance.

"Something pretty funny must have happened," he said.

"Not funny really," she said, finally controlling herself. "I just gave Bernice a frank bit of advice, and it shocked her so much I had to laugh."

"It's a nice change," he said. "Usually you come out gritting your teeth."

"I've had enough of that," she promised him. "Now I'm the one who takes care of herself. Bernice doesn't like it much."

"First thing you know she'll be leaving you," Jim suggested.

"That's what I'm hoping for," Edna said fervently.

The headwaiter showed them to their usual table in the large Wentworth dining room. The crowd was smaller than the last time, as it was later in the season and some of the summer visitors were already finding their way back to the city. Jim ordered lobsters for them, and then they began to talk.

He frowned. "I'm worried about Eric. He's drinking steadily and far too much."

She raised her eyebrows. "Still the same trouble?"

"You mean between him and Nancy?" Jim said. "Yes. I think that's really at the bottom of it."

"He's very fond of the girl, then?"

Jim looked at her solemnly. "I'd say he was desperately in love with her. And Eric is a very intense sort of person. He throws himself into everything with full force. He plays hard, works hard and in this case loves hard."

"What about Nancy?"

"She's tantalizingly cool, from the reports I've gotten," Jim went on. "I hear she's planning to join the cast of a touring show. She's leaving for New York at the end of the week when the playhouse closes here."

"I see," Edna said. "That wouldn't put Eric in a very good state of mind."

"I've never seen him drink like this before," Jim worried. "I'll be glad when the week is over."

"Eric is spoiled," she said. "He's gotten everything too easily. Now he thinks he should be able to reach out and grasp love the same way. It's a hard lesson for him to have to learn: that love isn't so readily available."

Jim's eyes met hers. "I've had to learn it."

She blushed. "Now you're talking nonsense."

"If I were a different type, like Eric, I'd have a reason to drink, too," he said. "You've been showing a lot of interest in that new doctor."

"You're imagining that!" she told him.

He shrugged. "You haven't given me as much of your time since he's come."

She gave him a faint smile. "I'm here with you now, aren't I?"

"How goes it with the doctor?" Jim wanted to know.

"I haven't seen anything of him since Uncle Charles went away," she said. "He's been awfully busy."

"Did he tell you about Dad's offer?"

She nodded. "Yes. As a matter of fact, he did."

Jim looked wise. "I hear he hasn't rejected it yet."

"I think he will."

"Don't be too sure."

"Then let's say I hope he will," Edna

said. "I'm sure your father regards him highly, and it's a flattering offer. But it's not for a man of Dr. Halliday's talents."

Jim showed surprise. "What's so wrong with the drug business? Your hospitals wouldn't get far without our supplies!"

"That's certainly true," she agreed. "But the position your father is offering Preston is just for company window dressing. He's worthy of more than that."

Jim winked at her. "We'll see what he decides."

Dinner was served, and then they danced. It was a good evening and passed too quickly. Before it seemed possible, it was twelve o'clock. The orchestra played a good night waltz, and the dance was over.

When Jim brought her home, she noticed that it was beginning to rain. Large drops began to patter against the windshield and on the car roof. Edna looked out into the darkness and gave a small shiver.

"There's something about a night like this," she said. "It's sort of weird. It won't be long till the big fall winds are here, and the storms."

He held his arm around her protectively. "I've tried to talk you into coming to Boston."

She smiled at him. "I might be there sooner than you think if I can persuade Bernice to sell the place."

"You really mean that?" he asked.

"Yes," she said. "I don't think I want to stay on in Farmingham. Too many memories."

"Come to Boston and build some new ones with me," he said lightly.

She looked at him with softly admiring eyes. "I am very fond of you, Jim. At least I know where I am with you. You've been my friend for a long time. You're so dependable."

He laughed. "I don't know whether I accept that as a compliment or not." He paused and said: "But we have been good friends. And I think friends owe each other frankness."

She gave him a startled look. "That's the second time someone has said that to me today."

Jim said: "Who, may I ask, was the first person?"

"No one important," she said. And then, correcting herself, she added: "I mean no one you know." She stared with far-away eyes at the windshield, watching the raindrops slide down and formlessly vanish.

"All right," Jim said. "We'll forget that.

Just give me a frank answer."

She looked at him again. "About what?"

"About us."

"The answer is the same. I still want to remain my own girl for a while, Jim." She said it quietly and with a touch of sadness in her voice.

"Then you haven't said yes to anyone else yet?"

She laughed. "Of course not. I've just told you."

He gave a sigh of relief. "Well, at least we've established that much." He looked at her fondly. "I suppose I'm silly, but I'm going to keep right on trying."

"I'd be devastated if you didn't," she assured him.

He cupped her small chin in his hand and drew her face close to his. Then, very deliberately, he kissed her.

They said good night, and she hurried inside between the raindrops. As she locked the door, she had the feeling that it would be an all-night rain. A storm had been predicted, and it was starting to beat down harder every minute. The combined weariness of the day and night caught up with her all at once. She turned and quickly started upstairs to bed.

Next morning it was still raining, and

she was glad to get a phone call from Mel Parker and the offer of a ride to the hospital. The blonde girl seemed terribly excited. She said: "I have a lot of news. But I'll wait until I see you. I'll be around in a few minutes."

It was about ten minutes later that Edna got into the car beside Mel and saw that the blonde girl's angular face was glowing with excitement. "Have you heard about Eric Boone?" Mel asked.

Edna was suddenly alert. "No. What is it this time?"

Mel was serious. "I'm afraid he's really done a job of it," she said, watching the traffic ahead.

"Don't keep me in suspense," Edna begged. "What's he done?"

Mel kept her eyes straight in front of her as she waited for a light to change. "He had a terrible smash-up. The little Carrington girl was with him when it happened. The car is a total loss."

"What about them?"

The blonde nurse shook her head. "They were both admitted to the hospital in the early morning hours. After three, I think. Both of them are in bad shape. Eric is on the second floor, and Nancy Carrington is in 306. Dr. Penny's stroke patient died after you left yesterday, so the room was free."

"What happened?" Edna wanted to know. "Did they hit another car, or what?"

Mel shrugged. "I guess he must have been drunk. He drove over a fifty-foot embankment. They should both be dead by now. They're lucky!"

"That depends," Edna said quietly, "on how badly injured they are. I wonder why Jim didn't get in touch with me."

"One of the night nurses phoned me," Mel said. "She said Jim had been at the hospital all night. He's probably still there and counts on seeing you when you come in."

It turned out that Mel was right. Jim was waiting for her in the lobby when she arrived. She took one glance at his pale face and the dark circles under his eyes and knew that he'd had a sleepless, tormented night.

She grasped his arm. "I've just heard. How are they?"

"About the same," he said, staring at her with dazed eyes. "Dad's in Boston. I've talked to him on the phone. He's driving down."

"Good," she said. "Have you had anything to eat?"

He shook his head. "I'm not hungry."

"You're dead on your feet," she told him. "You've got to take hold of yourself. You want to be in some kind of shape when your father gets here."

"I'll be all right." He shook his head like a prizefighter trying to come out of a daze. "It's just that everything's happened so suddenly."

She pulled on his arm. "You're coming down to the cafeteria with me. You can at least have some coffee."

Later, as they sat at one of the tables over coffee and toast, he pieced together the bits of he story that he knew "They had a quarrel backstage in the theatre," he said. "Then they showed up at the Wentworth after we left, but the bar was closed. Eric didn't need liquor, anyway. They said he was drunk and had a bottle in the pocket of his topcoat. Quite a few people saw it."

"What about Nancy?" Edna asked.

He shook his head. "I don't think she'd had a drink. The people at the hotel said she seemed sober enough and was trying to get him out of there."

"It couldn't have been long after that that they had the accident," she said.

"Maybe an hour later," Jim said. "Probably he drove around or parked somewhere before it happened."

"Since it wasn't a collision, he must have gone into a skid on the wet road," Edna reasoned, sipping her coffee.

Jim paused with his cup midway from the table. "No," he said. "The State Police don't seem to think so. The car just seemed to head over the edge of the road. There were no skid marks, no sign of the brakes being applied. They think something like a faulty tie-rod might have caused it. If it had snapped, Eric would have had no control of the car. Or it could be that he was so drunk he fell asleep and drove straight off the road."

"Surely Nancy would have tried to stop him," Edna argued. "It must have been something that went wrong with the car itself."

Jim nodded. "It must have been. Maybe we'll never know."

She said: "It can't be that bad."

"They're both on the danger list," he said. "Dr. Halliday did an emergency operation on Eric after he came in. He's rallied once or twice to say a few words. Most of the time he's unconscious."

"What about Nancy?"

"Bad head injuries," Jim said. "She's not

179

spoken since she's been in the hospital. I've got private duty nurses with both of them now. I'm going to keep them on around the clock. If I can't find them here, we'll get them from Boston if we have to."

She sighed. "Time enough to worry about that later. Did Eric manage to say anything coherent in his few minutes of consciousness?"

"He asked about Nancy," Jim said. "I told him she was all right. Then he said he wanted to die. He said it twice."

Chapter Eleven

Edna stared at the big blond man with puzzled eyes. "That seems a strange thing for him to say," she observed. "Are you sure that's exactly what he said?"

He sighed. "I think so. He talked very slowly and said only a few words. I don't know why he should say such a thing. It doesn't sound like Eric."

"Unless," Edna said, "he blames himself for the accident."

Jim finished his coffee and put the cup down. "That could be." His face was grim. "The police will know something about that if they can find enough of the car in one piece to examine it properly."

"Well, they are both alive," she said. "They'll probably recover. I know it's a hard time for you, but try to keep your perspective."

He smiled at her weakly. "It's the worst thing I've ever been through. And I suppose Dad coming down won't make it any easier."

"You'll have to share the burden of it with him," she said. "And see that he doesn't upset himself too much."

"I'll go back to the lobby and wait," he said. "Dad should be here in another couple of hours."

She glanced at her wristwatch. "And I'm due on my floor." They both got up, and she went on to say: "I'll keep a close check on Nancy and let you know if there's any kind of change."

He looked at her gratefully. "I'm glad you're around, Edna."

She said: "You should have called me last night."

"I thought of it," he admitted as they went out to the elevator. "But I knew you needed your rest. And there was nothing you could do right then."

Jim got off on the main floor, and she stayed on until she came to the third. When she stepped out of the elevator, she saw Preston Halliday holding a serious conference with Head Nurse Emma Graham and Dr. Rodman.

She was more than a little surprised to see the squat Dr. Rodman at the hospital so early. Then she remembered how seriously he had been taking his position as the second in command during her uncle's absence and understood. When she approached the trio they had apparently come to the end of their discussion.

Dr. Rodman passed her on his way to the elevator. He bowed. "And how is our Miss Brayley this morning?" he wanted to know.

"Very well," she said. "I hear we have two bad accident cases."

His ugly face became solemn. "Yes. Dreadful thing! I don't know how his father will take it. Horace Boone is a patient of mine, you remember."

Edna found herself annoyed at his childish self-importance even in the face of tragedy. She said: "Yes, I do."

"He's coming to the hospital. On his way here now," Rodman went on in his pompous way. "We shall be lucky if the poor man doesn't end up in one of our beds again."

"How is the girl?" she asked.

Dr. Rodman shrugged. "About the same." He was obviously not too interested in Nancy's condition.

Edna nodded to Emma Graham and asked Preston Halliday: "How is she?"

The young doctor plainly showed his worry. "She's not responding as she could. There is brain damage, but no apparent pressure as there was with Eric Boone. I had to do an emergency on him when he was brought in."

"I heard about it," she said.

"He's coming along as well as can be expected now." The young doctor glanced in the direction of the corridor. "But I'm worried about the girl. If her condition doesn't change shortly, I think she should be taken into Boston by ambulance or helicopter."

"What about intercranial hemorrhage?" Edna asked. She knew this was one of the major dangers with brain injury.

Emma Graham smiled admiringly at Dr. Halliday and joined in the conversation. "He thought of that, my dear," she said. "He's already done an exploratory."

Edna realized she might have known that Preston would take this precaution.

She smiled at him. "You seem to have had a busy night."

"It was pretty grim for a time," he admitted.

Thinking of Nancy's beauty, she asked hesitantly: "Her face wasn't badly cut up?"

"No." He shook his head. "They both came off very well in that regard. Eric Boone needed some stitches in one cheek. Her face wasn't damaged at all. But she has suffered a cerebral concussion, and she isn't responding."

"Brain injuries are so hard to pinpoint," Emma Graham said. "We had a case like hers here a few years ago. An automobile accident, too, if I remember right. We thought she wouldn't live, but after a few days she came right out of it."

Preston Halliday nodded. "Most patients recover spontaneously. But if there should be some hidden pressure, I'd like to be sure. And that's a job for a specialist."

Edna asked: "Do you think it would be safe to move her to Boston?"

"She needs the kind of care they could give her there," he said. "The next best thing would be to have one of the specialists come down here."

The phone at the desk rang, and Emma Graham answered it. After a moment she turned to Edna. "It's a call for the Carrington girl's private nurse. Would you go in and tell her and relieve her while she takes it?"

"I'll go with you," Preston Halliday told Edna. "I want to take a look at her again before I go downstairs."

They walked down the corridor together. The young doctor's face mirrored his troubled state of mind.

She said: "I talked with Jim downstairs.

He's feeling very badly about it."

"I don't doubt it," Dr. Halliday said. "From what I hear, Eric has always been a problem for the family."

"He's been drinking a lot."

Dr. Halliday gave her a sharp look. "He certainly must have been drunk when he let this happen. Unless the car failed, he blacked out and went off the road."

She let him open the door of 306 and followed him in. The light in the room was subdued, and it was very quiet. The nurse by the bed was plump and white-haired and wore glasses. She looked up without speaking, then rose and came softly across the room to them.

Edna glanced toward the bed and the frail, deadly still figure under the sheets. Then she turned to the nurse, who had come close. "You're wanted on the phone," she whispered. "I'll take over until you come back."

The elderly nurse formed with her lips an unspoken: "Thank you." Then she carefully opened the door and went out, closing it after her softly.

Edna went over to the bed and watched as Preston Halliday touched the girl's wrist and checked her pulse. The waxen face on the pillow was lovely but bore only a faint resemblance to the striking beauty of Nancy Carrington. The injured girl's eyes were closed, and her breathing was slow and very faint.

Preston Halliday finished taking her pulse and then stood there for a time, studying the alarmingly still figure. At last he gave a brief nod to Edna and went out of the room. There was something eerie in the quietness and the girl's barely audible breathing.

Edna sat in the chair the private nurse had vacated and kept a close watch on the injured girl. She bent close to examine her more carefully and was transfixed by what seemed the shadowy twitch of a cheek muscle. It started and ended so quickly that she couldn't be sure she wasn't imagining things.

With a growing tension, she saw the cheek twitch a second time. And then the waxen features lost their blankness and took on an expression of sheer terror. Nancy's large blue eyes opened and stared up at Edna, and she let out a piteous cry of "No!"

Hypnotized by what was happening, Edna softly touched the injured girl's shoulder. She could feel the previously limp body tighten as Nancy stared up at the ceiling in wild-eyed fear.

Her lids fluttered, and she moved her gaze to Edna. The lips worked nervously, and she moaned: "He did it deliberately. Wanted to kill me! Did it to kill me! Kill me!" Her voice became louder and more hoarsely distinct with each word.

Then, as quickly as she'd regained consciousness, she lost it again; she went limp and still and her eyes closed. Edna removed her hand from Nancy's shoulder and stepped back, incredulous at what she'd just witnessed. As she stood there, dazed and horrified, the door opened and the private nurse returned. She went straight to the chair by the bed, seated herself and dismissed Edna with a smile.

Edna whispered to the woman: "She had a moment of consciousness just now. I'll let the doctor know."

The elderly nurse looked up at her with wondering eyes, and then glanced at her patient to see if there were any visible sign of improvement. There was none. Edna knew it would be pointless to explain further to the private nurse. She hurried across the room and slipped out quietly.

She rushed down the corridor and up to Head Nurse Graham at the desk. The head nurse had heard her running footsteps coming down the hallway, and now she glanced at her in a startled fashion.

"What has happened?" Mrs. Graham gasped. "You look green!"

"Call Dr. Halliday," Edna said excitedly. "Have him come back upstairs. It's urgent. Nancy just came to for a few minutes."

Without further question, Emma Graham put through the call. It seemed only a matter of seconds later that Preston Halliday emerged from the elevator.

He came to Edna quickly. "Did I understand right? The Carrington girl came to while you were in there?"

"For a few seconds at the most," she told him breathlessly. "She didn't know me, and she seemed terribly frightened."

Before she'd finished talking, he was halfway down to Nancy Carrington's room. Edna followed him as he went in. The atmosphere of the room was just the same as before. The patient was still and deathly quiet, and the stout nurse was seated calmly watching her.

Preston studied the motionless figure in the bed and whispered to Edna: "It looks as if she's slipped away again."

After this he took the nurse to a corner of a room and had a brief conversation with her in a low tone. Then he guided Edna lightly by the arm and led her out of the room.

In the corridor, he faced her with anxious eyes. "Just what did happen in there?"

She looked up at him and tried to find the right words. "It was just as I told you. She was conscious for a short period. She didn't recognize me, but she talked coherently enough. She seemed terrified, as if she were recalling the moment of the accident."

"What exactly did she say?" He shot the question at her.

Edna hesitated in an attempt to recall the exact words: "She moaned and then she said 'He did it deliberately. Wanted to kill me! Did it to kill me! Kill me!' Then she collapsed again."

Preston Halliday stared at her. "I thought so," he said in a low voice.

All at once Edna knew what he meant. But she wanted him to say it first. "You think it's important?"

He gave her a strange look. "It proves what I've suspected from the first. It wasn't a question of the car failing. Eric drove it off the road deliberately in a drunken fury, intending to kill both himself and the girl because she'd refused him."

Edna listened to the quiet intensity of his words and knew that they were true. It all fitted in. She remembered what Jim had said about Eric telling him he wanted to die. Yes, it all fitted in!

With a new awareness and fear in her eyes, she looked up at the young doctor's grave face. She said: "That means Eric is criminally responsible for what's happened."

Preston Halliday nodded. "If Nancy Carrington dies, it will be as if he murdered her."

"But he wanted to kill himself as well," she pointed out.

"He'll recover," the young doctor said. "I'm by no means certain about Nancy. If she dies, it isn't going to be easy for him." He paused and studied Edna with a piercing look. "You realize you will have to tell the police what you heard just now."

She recognized her responsibility in the matter, and it frightened her. She said: "It may not mean anything. She may have been mixed up."

"I know that," the young doctor agreed. "But there is a strong chance she was reliving the last moment before the accident. When the police try to reconstruct what happened, they'll want all possible information. You can't honestly hold back what you heard in there just now. It's for the police to decide its value."

Edna sighed. "Isn't it dreadful! You really think I should get in touch with the police now while they're both in this state?"

He shrugged. "It can wait a few hours or a day. Perhaps until your uncle gets back tomorrow. But you may as well face it. The authorities will have to be told."

"Maybe by that time she'll have regained consciousness permanently," Edna said hopefully, "and we'll learn the real truth."

"It's possible," Preston Halliday admitted. "This flash of clarity she had is a good sign."

She said: "You were with Eric when he first talked. Didn't he give his version of the accident and what caused it?"

"He seemed to be deliberately vague." The young doctor frowned. "And he did ramble on about wanting to die. Seems to fit in with what she told you."

Edna thought of a new development and raised her eyes to meet Preston's. "His father will be here shortly. Are you going to tell him what you suspect?"

"Probably not," he said. "Not until we've spoken to the police."

"May I tell Jim in confidence?"

His eyebrows rose. "You are very close, of course," he said, considering it aloud. Then he gave her a stern scrutiny. "How do you think he'd react? He might try to dissuade you from telling the authorities."

"Oh, no," she said, "Jim wouldn't ask me to do anything wrong."

"He might not see it our way," the young doctor warned. "He might feel he wanted to protect his brother. He might ask you to forget what you heard."

"Perhaps I'd better not mention it, then," she said, a tremor of doubt in her voice.

There was a cynical glint in Preston Halliday's eyes. "I leave that to you," he said. "But whatever happens, I'm a party to it now. And whatever you decide to do, I'll have to notify the police about what you told me."

Before she could find an answer, he had wheeled around and started along the corridor in the direction of the desk.

With a major effort Edna put the episode out of her mind and went about her regular work. David Danton was sitting up in his chair when she made her first call of the day on him.

The columnist's gaunt face was smiling

and he said: "I'm checking out of here to-morrow, Miss Brayley, just as soon as your uncle returns. Dr. Halliday told me I could."

"That's wonderful news," she told him.

"Yes," he said. "Dr. Halliday has arranged for my treatments on Thursday. So you see I'll not lose much time."

"I'm sure you'll feel better soon," she told him.

He sat back in the chair, a stately figure in the rich brown silk dressing gown in spite of his emaciated condition. The thin hands tightened on the arms of the chair as his eyes met hers. "When I came here," he said. "I was sure I was going to die. And I was badly frightened." He paused. "I still don't know definitely if I'll make it. But somehow I've become resigned. I've learned to live with my condition and fight it each day as well as I'm able. Win or lose, I think I'll be able to continue my fight. That's what I've gained from being here, Nurse."

She was touched by his frankness. Gazing at him with fond eyes, she said: "I hope you'll keep in touch with us."

"You shall hear from me," he promised. "I'm going to write something about this experience and all of you in my column.

And I'll be sending along personal notes to you and Dr. Brayley."

Edna smiled. "Just keep your present state of mind, and you'll be all right."

David Danton nodded. "Don't worry about me. It's my wife who presents the problem. She's let my illness drag her down terribly. I'm going to have to try to persuade her to get some psychiatric help. Perhaps Dr. Brayley can talk to her for me."

"I'm sure he'll be glad to," Edna assured the columnist.

Now it was time for her morning coffee break. Edna hurried down to the lobby in search of Jim Boone, but he was nowhere in sight. She went across to the receptionist and inquired about him.

The girl at the desk said: "His father arrived a little while ago, and they went up to the second."

Edna nodded her thanks and took the elevator to the second floor. She found Jim and his father in the small waiting room reserved for patients. Dr. Rodman was standing by the fat man's chair, a hand on the older Boone's shoulder.

As she came to the door of the room, she heard Rodman saying suavely, "Your son is getting the best of attention, Mr. Boone."

The fat man looked up at him, anxious and strangely white-faced. "You do think he will pull through?"

"Yes," Dr. Rodman said. "I'm sure of it."

"His back isn't injured?" Horace Boone quavered. "There's no chance of his being crippled?"

"Once he recovers from this brain injury," Dr. Rodman said, "there's nothing else to worry about beyond a few body cuts and bruises." He straightened up and took his hand from the millionaire's shoulder as Edna came in.

"Ah," he said, with a bland smile, "here is Nurse Brayley."

Jim came quickly forward. "What's the word on Nancy?"

She said: "It's still touch and go. She came to briefly while I was in with her."

Dr. Rodman also came over to her. "She did? That is a good sign!"

Edna shrugged. "I suppose so. She's slipped into unconsciousness again. It's my coffee break, and I wanted to let you know."

From his chair, old Horace Boone spoke up angrily. "Whatever happens to her, she deserves it! She caused all this!"

Startled by the violence of his outburst, both men turned to stare at him in surprise. The old man's pallor vanished as his face became purple and distorted with rage.

"You needn't look at me," he told them. "That's what I think, and I'm not afraid to say it. She deserves whatever happens to her!"

The injustice of it was too much for Edna. Before she could help herself, she'd taken a step toward Horace Boone and said indignantly: "You should be ashamed! If anyone is to blame for this, it's your son!"

The shrewd blue eyes in the fat face blinked at her malevolently. He gave her a look of disgust. "What right have you to concern yourself with this?"

Dr. Rodman intervened diplomatically before she replied. He gave her a warning nod. "Please, Miss Brayley! I must ask you to leave. My patient is in no fit state for this!"

Knowing this was true, she curbed her anger, turned and left the waiting room. As she walked down the hallway, she found herself trembling with rage and disgust.

"Edna, please!" It was Jim who called out to her.

She stopped and turned, and he came up quickly, his face showing a strange mingling of shock and annoyance.

He stared at her. "Whatever made you act that way in there?"

"What way?" she asked.

"You know what I mean," he said irritably. "Upset Father as you did just now."

She gave a small mirthless laugh. "Actually, he was the one who upset me."

Jim looked down sheepishly. "I know he shouldn't have talked the way he did. But you were almost as bad with your dramatics. You must realize he's badly upset and doesn't know what he's saying."

"I suppose I didn't act in a very professional way," she admitted wearily. "But I don't have to cater to him like his hired Dr. Rodman! I reserve the right to speak my mind!"

Jim's jaw dropped open in surprise. Then he recovered and swallowed angrily. "I hardly think this is the time for personalities. I don't know what to make of you, Edna. You were so decent when we talked this morning, such a help. Why do you act this way now?"

Her eyes met his, and she said in a firm voice: "I'm sorry if I hurt you, Jim. But I'm a little tired of everyone's sincere regard for the feelings of the Boone family. I think Nancy is important, too! And I intend to go on thinking so. When she was conscious for those few minutes, she told me something I think you should know."

He stared at her. "What should I know?"

"She accused Eric of deliberately wrecking the car to kill them both. If she dies, he's criminally responsible for what's happened!"

There was a long moment of silence. Then he said quietly: "What do you intend doing with that information?"

Chapter Twelve

Edna said: "Naturally, I'll have to tell the police."

He opened his eyes wide. "You'd repeat what are quite likely the demented ravings of a sick girl. Do you think anyone will place any credence in them?"

"That's for me to judge," she said quietly.

He paused, then asked: "Who else knows this?"

"Dr. Halliday," she said.

"I see," he said quietly. "I suppose he goes along with the idea of repeating this nonsense to the police."

"Yes," she said, "he does. And it doesn't have to be nonsense."

His expression became pleading. "Edna, can't you forget this?"

She looked at him curiously. "Would you respect me if I did?"

"That doesn't enter into it."

"I think that it does."

"I see." He set his mouth in a firm line.

"I'm sorry, Jim," she said sincerely.

He stared at her for a moment with the old sullen expression she knew so well, then wheeled around and strode back down the corridor. She watched after him until he turned into the waiting room again, then continued to the cafeteria for coffee.

Afterwards, when she went upstairs, Nurse Graham gave her the message. She said: "I've been trying to reach you. Dr. Halliday wants you in his office right away."

She knew as she took the elevator to the main floor again that he wanted to talk about Nancy. When she entered the young doctor's office and saw him behind his desk facing a line of chairs in which Jim, Horace Boone and Dr. Rodman solemnly arrayed, she was sure it wasn't going to be a pleasant interview.

The men rose as she came in, and Preston Halliday gave her a dreary smile and indicated the chair beside his desk. "Please sit down," he said.

It was like some ridiculous ritual, she thought as she took the chair. The others resumed their seats, and Horace Boone glared at her.

He said: "We're all very much upset, Miss Brayley."

She said: "I'm sorry."

Jim studied his nails and avoided looking at her. Horace Boone turned to Dr. Rodman in an unspoken appeal for support.

The stout little doctor forced a hard smile and, leaning forward toward Edna, said: "I'm sure this can be settled without any fuss. You don't want to be accused of a breach of professional etiquette, do you, Miss Brayley?"

She shook her head. "No, I wouldn't want that."

Dr. Rodman brightened and glanced briefly at the old millionaire before he again gave his attention to her. "I was sure you'd feel that way."

"The question is," she said, meeting his eyes, "just what would constitute a breach of professional etiquette in this instance?"

The squat doctor gave Preston Halliday a worried glance and then forced a laugh. "I don't think that presents any puzzle. Does it, Dr. Halliday?"

Preston Halliday was watching the proceedings with a stoical expression. "I'd prefer to hear Miss Brayley's views," he said.

Dr. Rodman looked at her. "Well, my dear?"

She took a deep breath. "I think we're all wasting time," she said, "and worrying about the wrong things. The important thing, as I see it, is that they both recover. If Nancy dies, I'll feel obliged to tell the police what she said to me."

Horace Boone sighed deeply. "Do you think it fair to threaten me this way?"

"I don't regard it as threat," she told him quietly.

Dr. Rodman was his usual pompous self. "I must warn you, Miss Brayley, that I shall report your actions to your uncle. You are deliberately causing these people mental anguish. And Mr. Boone is a patient in my care."

"It's not pleasant to find myself in this position," Edna said. "But since I am, there's only one course I can take."

"How do you feel about this, Dr. Halliday?" Horace Boone turned his attention to the young doctor. "Surely you don't agree?"

Preston Halliday sat back in his chair. "I'm sorry, sir," he said, "but I find myself in complete agreement with Miss Brayley."

No one spoke for a moment.

Finally Horace Boone stood up, plainly worried. He said: "I seldom make a mistake in a man, Halliday. But it seems I have in my judgment of you. I have even offered you a position with my firm. I presume you realize I may wish to reconsider that offer now?"

Preston Halliday stood up with an ironic smile. "I'm not surprised at all. You see, I've encountered several situations not unlike this in the past. I'm not altogether a naïve idealist. In any case, I have decided to refuse your offer. It isn't for me."

Edna felt her spirits soar as he said this with quiet dignity. At least that problem was settled. Out of this dreadful situation one good thing had emerged. She had prayed from the first that Preston Halliday wouldn't accept the job with the Boone company. It would have been the end of his career.

The old millionaire looked frustrated. "I see," he said. "It is my opinion you're acting hastily and with poor judgment. You surely don't think this ridiculous story would carry any weight? Let me assure you that I'll fight it with all the means at my disposal. And they are considerable!"

With that he turned and lumbered out of the office. The other two followed after him. Jim glanced back and nodded to Edna as a show of friendliness. Then he joined his father and Dr. Rodman in the corridor.

Preston Halliday grinned at the nurse, came over and took her firmly by the arm. "Good girl!" he said. "I was proud of you."

She gave him a skeptical look. "Horace Boone can be a nasty enemy."

"I've made a career of lining up nasty enemies," he assured her.

"Well," she said, "anyway, he knows

where we stand. I hope my uncle approves."

"He's bound to," Dr. Halliday assured her.

The next morning, as Charles Brayley sat in his office and heard their story out, he did. He'd summoned both Dr. Halliday and Edna for an early morning discussion of the matter. Now he laid his hands on his desk with a sigh and looked from one to the other.

"I'll certainly back you up in this," he said gravely, "although my real hope is that I don't have to. How are they this morning?"

Preston Halliday said: "Eric is much better, and Nancy is at least holding her own, although she's still unconscious."

Dr. Brayley frowned. "I'll make a few calls to Boston this morning. Maybe we can get a man down here. This could develop into one of those cases where the patient stays unconscious for months. I don't like it."

The young doctor stood up. "If you don't need me any longer, sir, I'd like to go back upstairs and take a look at Miss Carrington again."

Charles Brayley waved him off. "Go ahead," he said. "Come by and let me know how she is."

Preston Halliday smiled at Edna as he went out. She returned the smile and then spoke to her uncle. "When all this is settled," she said, "I'm thinking of moving to Boston."

He looked at her with surprise. "Isn't that a new idea?"

"In a way," she agreed. "I don't feel I want to go on living with Bernice."

The bald man nodded in understanding. "I've expected to hear you say that for some time. I know it hasn't been easy. But do you think the solution is to leave Farmingham and the hospital?"

"I like being at the hospital," she said. "And I'd miss you terribly. But I must make some sort of break."

"How about coming to live with your aunt and me?" he suggested.

"That would hardly be fair" — she shook her head — "however appealing I might find it. You've built up a way of life over the years. I'd be a disturbing factor in a dozen different ways. Let me work things out myself."

He smiled at her indulgently. "Think it over carefully. That's all I ask."

There was an air of tension in the hospital that even her uncle's return did not dispel. She heard that Horace Boone and

"Jim mentioned it."

"Have you seen him?" Bernice gave her a searching look. Edna was sure her stepmother was suspicious that something had happened between her and Jim.

"I've been terribly busy," she alibied. "I think he's called at the hospital several times with his father."

"I see," Bernice said as if unconvinced. She went into the living room and sat down. "Well, I suppose we'd better get our talk over."

Edna sank into a plain chair by the door. Her tone was weary as she asked: "What is it now?"

Bernice gave her a catty smile. "It seems I'm neither as old or as much on the shelf as you seem to think. Elliot has asked me to marry him."

Edna sat forward in surprise. "How wonderful!"

"Not right away, of course," Bernice added quickly. "But he is very serious, and he wants me to go back to New York. He does television work there in the winter. He thinks I should take a job and live there until we're married."

Edna couldn't believe the good news. It was the answer to her problem. She said: "Of course you're going?"

Bernice hunched on the divan. "Well, I've given it a lot of thought. Elliot is a wonderful person, and I mightn't get another chance like this. And then you seem so anxious to break up this home!" Her tone was vindictive as she said this.

"I've been thinking about us both," Edna put in quickly, "about what would be best for our futures."

"Well, it's settled," Bernice said. "I'm starting to gather some of my things up now. Elliot is going to drive me back with him on Saturday. We can put the furniture into the hands of the local auctioneer and the house with the real estate people. The paintings can be handled by the same gallery who are selling them now."

These were all terms agreeable to Edna. She nodded. "That will be fine." And then, as a precautionary move, she added: "I'll have a lawyer friend of Dad's act for me."

Bernice raised her eyebrows. "You think that's necessary?"

"Unless we're strictly legal about it," Edna warned, "we could run into all sorts of trouble and delays."

Bernice considered this bleakly. "I suppose you're right."

"One thing," Edna said. "I want Dad's portrait."

Her stepmother shrugged. "Well, I have had an offer of three thousand for it."

"You can take my fifteen hundred out of my share of the house," Edna told the blonde woman. "I want to keep it."

"I'm sure it makes no difference to me," Bernice said very casually. "I'll be starting a new life."

Edna got up, went over to her and kissed her on the cheek. "I hope you'll be very happy. I honestly do."

Bernice's blue eyes opened wide as she stared up at her. "You're a strange girl. I've often felt you didn't like me."

Edna smiled. "Let's admit it hasn't always been easy. But I think we've done as well as any two people could have in our circumstances."

"Yes," Bernice said. "I suppose we have. Well, I must finish my work." She got up and went back to cleaning out the closet.

"And I must have my nap," Edna said.

She was on the bed with her eyes closed, but not asleep, when Elliot Roger came by to pick up Bernice. She heard the sound of their voices downstairs for a time, and then the door closed after them and they were gone. A deep sigh of relief escaped her as she realized that in a few days Bernice would have left forever. It was wonderful to know that she'd soon be free.

Later in the evening she phoned her uncle. When she had him on the line, she said: "I've been thinking over your offer, Uncle Charles. If you still feel the same way about it, I would like to live with you for a few months."

"Your aunt and I have discussed the very matter this evening," he told her warmly. "Your room will be ready for you any time you decide to come."

Next morning at the hospital, Nurse Graham signaled her just before coffee break time. When she went over to the desk, the head nurse said: "Your uncle wants to see you in his office."

Thinking it had something to do about her going to live with him, Edna hurried along the passage to his office with a carefree feeling. When she went in, she was surprised to find him sitting there with Mrs. David Danton.

He stood up. "Mrs. Danton has something to say to you, Edna," he told her. And with a nod, he left them alone in the office.

The columnist's wife glanced at Edna with a troubled expression. "Miss Brayley, I'm here to ask your forgiveness. My husband and I had a long talk last night. There are some things I understand now that I have never fully understood before."

Edna said, "There's no need for this."

Mrs. David Danton shook her head. "Every need! David knows he may not get well. No one has to tell him that. He made this quite clear to me. But he is ready to fight for the time he has left. In the face of his courage, I must stop feeling sorry for myself."

Edna was touched by the change in the woman. She said, "The radiation therapy may do wonders for him."

"I hope so." Mrs. Danton sighed. "All I want to do now is to make every day David has left as good and happy as possible. He told me that he felt badly about my behavior toward you. I don't want him to worry about it. That is why I'm here."

"I understand," Edna said.

Mrs. Danton got up. "Thank you. I owed you an apology. We're leaving for Boston this afternoon."

Edna saw her to the door. "We'll all want to know how he is."

The older woman nodded. "You'll hear from us. Either David or I will write and let you know how things are."

It was a happy beginning for the day. Edna hoped the columnist would improve, and she also wished there might be some good word about Nancy. It came shortly after lunch, when Preston Halliday emerged from Nancy's room with a delighted smile.

"She's conscious," he told Edna and Head Nurse Graham. "She finally came around. If she keeps improving this way, we have nothing more to worry about."

The word spread swiftly through the hospital corridors, and it helped to ease the general tension they'd all felt since the accident. The reports continued to be encouraging, and Edna felt a great load slip from her. If Nancy got well, she need never tell the police what the girl had said in that dramatic moment. It would then be up to Nancy whether she wanted to tell anyone or not.

When it came time to go home, she found Jim Boone in the hospital lobby waiting for her. The big blond man approached her with a sheepish smile. "Can I talk to you for a few minutes?"

She stared up at him. "I suppose so," she said. "There's really nothing to say."

"I think there is," he said.

They went outside and stood in the late afternoon sun. Edna moved to the far end of the stone entrance steps where they could talk without being in anyone's way and without anyone overhearing their conversation. She stared out at the hospital lawn and trees, her back to him.

He said: "Eric's a walking patient now. He's up in Nancy's room at this moment, asking her forgiveness and promising her he'll never quarrel again about sharing her with her career. I thought you'd like to know. He really does love her."

"That's good," Edna said without turning. "Is that all?"

"What about us?" His tone was pleading. "Can't we at least pick up where we left off?"

She shook her head. "I think we'd better forget about us, Jim."

He was silent for a moment. "I see," he said. "I think it was all settled before this happened. Well, I wish you both happiness."

When she looked around, he was gone. She had the feeling that this would be the last intimate moment they would ever know. Should they cross paths again, it would be the casual meeting of strangers. A big part of her short lifetime had gone into their romance, and it wasn't surprising that the knowledge that it was over caused her eyes to fill with tears. She hurried down the broad stone steps and started home.

Sunday was another fine day, and it was her first free day in the house alone. She intended to move over to her uncle's on Sunday evening, and she was busy packing a few of her personal things when the phone rang. It was Preston Halliday.

"I hear you're all alone. How about having dinner with another lonely party?"

"It sounds grand," she told him. "But I'd appreciate your coming early and helping me with some of my belongings. I'm moving tonight."

"I'll be right over," he promised.

She was in the dining room taking down her father's portrait when the doorbell rang. She let him in, and he helped her wrap the portrait in cardboard to protect it. Glancing up at him, she thought he looked very handsome and protective in his gray trousers and dark sports jacket.

Smiling down at the partially wrapped portrait, she said: "The most important man in my life."

Then his arm was around her, and he looked into her face with a happy glow in his brown eyes. "How about allowing me to become the second most important?"

In answer she offered him her lips. And as he took her in his arms for a long kiss, she lost her last feeling of insecurity.